HIDDEN AGENDAS

TRUE VISION SERIES, VOL I

AJIT & ANIL

Srishti
Publishers & Distributors

Srishti Publishers & Distributors
A unit of AJR Publishing LLP
212A, Peacock Lane
Shahpur Jat, New Delhi – 110 049

editorial@srishtipublishers.com

First published by
Srishti Publishers & Distributors in 2023

10 9 8 7 6 5 4 3 2 1

This is a work of fiction. The characters, places, organisations and events described in this book are either a work of the author's imagination or have been used fictitiously.

Any resemblance to people, living or dead, places, events, communities or organisations is purely coincidental.

The author asserts the moral right to be identified as the author of this work.

Printed and bound in India.

To our beloved families, who have been our greatest support and inspiration throughout this journey.

To the ones who encouraged us to dream, even when the road seemed uncertain, and who believed in us long before we believed in ourselves.

Your unwavering love, patience, and faith have been the foundation of this series.

We dedicate this work to you for the laughter, the late-night talks, the endless cups of tea, and the gentle reminders that we are never alone in this journey.

This book is a reflection of your love, and we are forever grateful.

Praise for the book

True Vision is truly engaging and exciting.

—**Sashi Kumar**, Founder, Asianet & Chairman, Asian College of Journalism

Gripping Stories that make a thrilling read.

—**Times Of India**

Ajit & Anil have mastered the art of blending fact with fiction. This a 'Ready to Shoot' book.

—**ANI**

A Thrilling First Volume.

—**The Print**

Contents

Foreword

Blending real-life events with cinematic storytelling, Ajit Menon and Anil Verma's latest release, Hidden Agendas, creates an immersive experience that combines truth with the dramatic flair of fiction. With gripping stories set against a backdrop of family feuds, political intrigue and the dark underbelly of seemingly peaceful lives, this book makes a riveting read. An intricately woven world of intrigue, deceit and heart-pounding suspense awaits readers.

Published by Srishti Publishers & Distributors, this book is not just about uncovering secrets - it is a journey that will keep you hooked from the first page to the last. A gripping and masterfully told collection that reflects the best of modern crime fiction and gives you a visual feel as you read.

—The Times of India

Author's Note

"Storytelling is an art.
If you can't visualise what
you are reading, then it's trash." – Ajit & Anil.

Cinematic tales weave the fabric of reality with the threads of imagination, creating a tapestry that transcends both truth and fiction. When captured in cinematic style, stories bridge the gap between reality and creative imagination.

These narratives captivate readers by transforming true events into compelling, visually rich experiences that evoke deep emotions and provide new perspectives.

By blending factual accuracy with artistic storytelling, these stories offer a unique and immersive experience that resonates with the authenticity of real life while embracing the dramatic flair of cinema.

When you read, you feel as though you are watching a movie.

……Read on

Aravani

A term for the transgender individuals of communities who consider themselves as females trapped in male bodies. Aravani is a widely recognised term in the state of Tamil Nadu.

Prologue

"Aravani" is a psychological thriller that delves into the enigmatic journey of Sub Inspector Pritika Mudaliyar, a resilient transgender who defied societal norms in Tamil Nadu and became a famous Police Officer.

The story is inspired by the real life journey of Tamil Nadu's first transgender police officer—Prithika Yashini.

***

Life moved tranquilly in the sleepy town of Attayampatti, in Salem-Tamil Nadu.

Salem played a prominent part in India's history. During revolutionary times, a party of Salem patriots made the first armed resistance against the British authority at the North Bridge in 1775.

Situated southwest of Salem city, Attayampatti was known for its *murukku*, a snack made of rice flour. Most residents made murukku and sold it in front of their houses. The townspeople were close knit, intertwined in a web of familiarity and routine.

That was until the winter of 2023, when a shocking crime shattered the peace, leaving the community reeling in horror.

Chapter 1

It all began on a cold December morning in 2023 when Jeisy Jhonson, a thirty-year-old local English schoolteacher, was found dead in her home. Her neighbour, Mrs Manorama, discovered the body when she noticed Jeisy hadn't left for work. Concerned, she knocked on Jeisy's door, but there was no answer. She tried the door handle and realised that the door was unlocked; Mrs Manorama entered, calling out for her friend, only to be met with an eerie silence. As she ventured further inside, she found Jeisy lying on the bed. Initially, she thought Jeisy was sleeping, but on closer examination, she found she wasn't breathing. Panic-stricken, Mrs Manorama called the Attayampatti police station and spoke to the dispatch desk. Attayampatti Police Station in-charge SP Rajiv Kulasekaran instructed thirty-two-year-old Sub Inspector Prithika Mudaliyar to take charge of the case.

SI Prithika arrived at the scene with her second-in-command, head constable Divij Acahaari, and quickly secured the area, ensuring no evidence was tampered with. Jeisy's house was modest, reflecting her simple lifestyle. Upon entering, Prithika noticed the door was unlocked. She examined it and said to Acahaari, "No signs of forced entry. If this is murder, then she knew her killer."

"You haven't even seen the body, and you are already talking about murder?" asked Acahaari, irritated. Prithika's sharp eyes scanned the room. Jeisy's body bore no visible wounds, and there was no sign of a struggle. Apart from the open book lying on the coffee table next to the bed and a lonely teacup in the kitchen sink, everything was in its place: neat and clean. The scene was eerily calm—almost too calm.

Prithika picked up the book with gloved hands and looked at the cover. It was a spy novel called *The Puppeteer.* As she flipped through the pages, her eyes stopped on page 84. The last sentence on the page was underlined with a blue pen: *'No day is so bad it can't be fixed with a nap.'*

Prithika gazed at Jeisy's serene, sweet face and her still, peaceful body, then turned to Acahaari and said, 'She truly looks like she's taking a peaceful nap.'

"Looks like she died in her sleep. Heart attacks have become very common in youngsters nowadays," said Acahaari.

Prithika handed *The Puppeteer* to Acahaari and said, "She does not look the types who would be interested in espionage or crime stories."

"What type does she look like?" asked Acahaari sarcastically, as he bagged the book for forensics.

"The type that reads contemporary romance. Stories that tug at the heartstrings and make you sob," she retorted, pointing at a bookshelf near a small couch by the window. It was filled with romantic novels.

Then she turned to Acahaari and said wryly, "This is not a heart attack. It is murder."

Chapter 2

Flashback

It was early morning, 5:00 a.m. The weather was foggy, and it was raining heavily in Attayampatti. Priest Arumugam, the pujari of the old Shiva temple on the outskirts of Attayampatti, was an early riser, and he was already inside the sanctum sanctorum to bathe the deity when he heard the sound of a bike outside. He casually looked out and saw a man park the bike outside the temple. The man had a bundle tied to his chest. He climbed the temple steps, untied the bundle, and left it on the floor at the entrance. Then he bowed to the deity, whispered a prayer, returned to his bike, and rode off into the foggy morning. Arumugam had a clear view of the rider. He put down the mug of water, walked up to the bundle on the steps, and looked at it. Inside was a fair, beautiful thirty-day-old infant. Despite the fog, the cold, and the rain lashing heavily outside, the child was fast asleep. Arumugam picked up the child, wondering who could abandon such a beautiful baby when his eye fell on the baby's private part. "Oh my god, Aravani," he whispered.

"What do I do?" Arumugam asked himself. After thinking long and hard, he made his decision. He covered the baby nicely in a warm shawl, held it close to his chest, took an umbrella, and walked towards the town.

***

Postman Ayyaswamy Mudaliyar was in his early fifties but way more intelligent than most people in town. He guessed the reason when he saw Priest Arumugam so early on his doorstep with an infant in his arms. He stepped aside and let Arumugam in. Once seated, Arumugam looked at Ayya and said, "Everyone in this town ridicules you because you are sterile and single. But you take all the humiliation with a smile and a prayer. Well, the lord has heard your prayers."

Arumugam handed the infant to Ayyaswamy, saying, "You were not destined to produce a child because you were destined to raise the lord himself."

"But the infant is an Aravani," he protested.

"No. This is Ardhanareeshvari—Shiva & Shakti merged into one. The child was delivered to me in the temple, which is the lord's wish. I am but a messenger. Mahadev wants you to raise him." Arumugam explained everything to Ayyaswamy. Pointing to the infant, he said, "You both are born in suffering. But together, you will find joy and happiness. Raise her like your daughter. Educate her and give her a life she will be proud of. This is the lord himself, so do not be afraid of society. Brave everything, and she will make you proud one day."

Arumugam knew the local registrar and ensured the adoption went smoothly. A week later, the infant was named in a quiet ceremony attended by the registrar, Ayyaswamy, and Arumugam. After the puja, Ayyaswamy held her close and whispered her name thrice in her ear: "Prithika, Prithika, Prithika." Prithika meant 'Flower'—a flower that had blossomed in the sterile and barren world of Ayyaswamy. Over the years, Ayyaswamy provided Prithika with the best education at the local private missionary schools. Though Prithika excelled in class and was a favourite of the teachers and faculty, she could not escape the taunts and humiliation for being an Aravani. While everyone made fun of her in school, Ayyaswamy stood by her like a rock and helped her overcome her fears. As she grew older, she realised the trauma Ayyaswamy was undergoing, both as an impotent man and the father of an Aravani. This led her to be even more respectful of Ayyaswamy. As Arumugam had predicted, they faced the world together and became very close to each other.

When Prithika entered college, things started changing for them. Ayyaswami was promoted to postmaster as his superior died of a heart attack, and no one else was willing to come to Attayampatti. Two years later, Ayyaswamy won a lottery of Rs 40 lakhs. He used the money to build a house for themselves. Soon, the news about Prithika being a lucky omen for Ayyaswamy travelled, and the locals started looking at Ayyaswamy with renewed respect. But as per local tradition, they still invited Prithika to their homes as an Aravani to bless their children. Ayyaswamy resented it, but Prithika said, "At least this way, no one will ignore us, Appa." Prithika knew the town people treated her like an Aravani, but she was content as long as it allowed them to live peacefully in society.

Drawn towards social sciences and humanities, Prithika soon completed her studies in Sociology, Psychology, and Criminology. Strangely adamant about joining the Police force, Prithika, after her studies, came first in her Sub Inspector exam, conducted by the state government and underwent one year of training at the Police Academy. A favourite of everyone at the academy, during her posting interview, the board asked her, "So, where do you want to get posted?"

"Attayampatti, sir," she said with a firmness that surprised them.

"Attayampatti it is," they said with a smile.

Chapter 3

Twenty-four hours after being assigned to investigate Jeisy's death, Prithika walked into DSP Rajiv Kulasekaran's office and said, "This is a premeditated murder, sir,"

DSP Rajiv Kulasekaran, a handsome man known for his flirtatious behaviour despite being in his late fifties, looked up from his desk. He was a widower—his wife had died early in their marriage, and he had chosen not to remarry. Kulasekaran had asked for a transfer from the Head Office to Attayampatti, stating it was his home town and he wanted to retire at a peaceful place. But it had hardly been six months since he took charge when Jeisy was murdered. As such, Kulasekaran was tough on his team, and known for his quick temper and irritability. Now, after hearing about Jeisy's murder, he had become more irritable. While all his subordinates feared him, the only person who could stand up to Kulasekaran was Prithika; strangely, the two got along well.

"How do you say that?" asked Kulasekaran, looking irritated.

"I saw the toxicology report. She died of Cyanide poisoning. And cyanide is a substance rarely found outside of industrial use."

"Cyanide is still used as a pesticide to control ants, certain bacteria, insects, and rodents in residential and commercial areas. Some people in Attayampatti still use it. You can find it in all the older homes," argued Kulasekaran.

"I agree, but that is Sodium Cyanide, which is also capable of killing, but in Jeisy's case, Potassium Cyanide powder was used. Page 84 of the book, *The Puppeteer,* was sprinkled with Cyanide powder and a sentence was underlined on the page. The killer made sure the victim opened the page, exposing her to the deadly poison. Traces of Cyanide were also found on the victim's lips. She may have touched the page and unwittingly licked her finger to turn other pages."

"Possible. The big question is, who would want a simple, sweet, and loving English teacher dead?" asked Kulasekaran.

"I don't know, but I will find out," said Prithika.

"Good work. Keep me informed of your progress. If you need any help, let me know," said Kulasekaran.

"Thank you for all your support, sir. I appreciate what you are doing for me," she said gratefully. "Please don't thank me. I am just doing my duty. You do your best to make Ayyaswami proud," said Kulasekaran. Kulasekaran knew Prithika's adopted father, Ayyaswami, well and had also visited her home a few times for drinks and dinner with him.

***

As the investigation unfolded, Prithika and Acahaari delved into Jeisy's life. They found she was well-liked by her students and colleagues and had no known enemies. However, as they dug deeper, they uncovered a secret side of her life that painted a different picture. Jeisy was having an affair with a married doctor, Dr Suryakantam Udayar. Their relationship had been discreet, but not for long. One day, Udayar's wife, Simran, found out. Known for her temper and jealousy, Simran created a scene at home, which even the neighbours overheard.

Prithika interviewed Udayar, who appeared distraught over Jeisy's death. He admitted to the affair, said it was a short relationship borne out of a moment of weakness but denied any involvement in her murder. His alibi—being at his clinic on the day of the murder—seemed airtight. On the contrary, Simran's demeanour was cold and detached, and failed to convince Prithika about her whereabouts at the time of the murder. There was something about Simran not sitting right with Prithika. Further investigation revealed that Simran had recently purchased potassium cyanide powder. This raised suspicions further.

Prithika decided to dig deeper into Simran's past and discovered that she and Udayar were college friends. She also learnt that Simran was highly possessive of Udayar and had a history of violent behaviour and threats toward his girlfriends during their college days. An FIR was also lodged against her for beating up one of Udayar's college girlfriends at Lucknow Medical College after suspecting her of having a crush on him.

It became clear to Prithika that Simran had a motive, but she needed more to make an arrest. "The effects of potassium cyanide are instant and occur within minutes of contact. The victim loses consciousness, and brain death eventually follows. The victim may suffer convulsions, and death is caused by cerebral hypoxia. The killer ensured the book reached Jeisy, and that she read page 84. The death happened inside the house. The door was open, which means the killer was there when the victim died. After Jeisy's death, the killer placed her on the bed to make it look like she died in her sleep," she said to herself.

***

Prithika and Acahaari interrogated Simran. During the interrogation, she told them she was aware of Surya's betrayal and had confronted him, but he never admitted to it. So, she met Jeisy at her residence and pleaded with her to stay out of Surya's life.

"I begged her to leave my husband, and she agreed. I thanked her profusely and left. I didn't kill her," said Simran.

"You were the last person to meet with Jeisy. Your fingerprints were on the book by her bedside, and the book had traces of Cyanide. Jeisy died of Cyanide poisoning. According to Acahaari, the local chemist said you purchased Potassium Cyanide powder a day before Jeisy's death. Everything points at you, so you better confess," she said.

"Everything you said is true, but I didn't kill Jeisy. I had no reason to—she agreed to leave Surya. Please, believe me," Simran pleaded.

Though Simran refused to accept that she was guilty of murder, Prithika moved ahead with the chargesheet. The trial was swift. Simran's motive, her confessions of meeting Jeisy, her fingerprints on the book, the Cyanide powder found in her house and the traces of it on page 84, and the cause of death being Cyanide ingestion left little doubt of her guilt in the judge's mind. At the end of the month-long trial, Simran was sentenced to life imprisonment, leaving Udayar to grapple with the consequences of his infidelity and the loss of both his lover and wife. Humiliated and indirectly blamed for his wife's actions, Udayar took a transfer and left Attayampatti.

The Jeisy murder case catapulted Prithika to fame, turning her into a hero overnight.

Congratulations poured into Ayyaswamy's house, and the local women started addressing Prithika as Shakti. Despite the respect and the fame, Prithika felt a sense of unease that she couldn't erase. Throughout the case, she had never been fully convinced that Simran was the killer. The look in Simran's eyes when she was led to prison haunted her. Every night, Simran came in her dreams, pleading, 'I am innocent.'

In the aftermath of Jeisy's murder, Attayampatti struggled to come to terms with the tragedy. Once a haven of peace, the town was now filled with whispered fears and lingering sorrow.

Chapter 4

Three weeks passed, but the memory of Jeisy's murder still lingered in Prithika's mind. Unable to get over her nightmares, she confided in Acahaari. "Somehow, I have a nagging feeling we convicted an innocent woman," she said as they sat at their favourite tea shop.

"Look, we didn't convict her. We just shared the evidence and the motive. The judge convicted her. So, stop feeling guilty unless you can prove otherwise," he said.

They were on their second cup of tea when a news report on TV about a murder in Muthiapuram, Tuticorin, caught their attention. Tuticorin was a port city famous for pearl fishing and shipping activities, salt production, and other related businesses. Muthiapuram was a remote, sleepy village in the Tuticorin district, perched in the midst of nowhere. It was one of the most peaceful places on earth, and a murder there was unthinkable. But, more than the village or the murder, what caught Prithika's attention was the victim and the method of the murder. The victim was Tamini Gounder, an English schoolteacher at a local government school. She had died of Cyanide poisoning. The local cops were yet to trace the source of the Cyanide and how it was administered to the victim. Watching the news, Prithika was suddenly reminded of Simran. She looked at Acahaari and asked, "Where did Udayar say he was getting transferred to?"

"Muthiapuram," whispered Acahaari with a shocked look.

Prithika looked at Acahaari and said, "We must catch him before he commits a third murder."

"What do we do? Muthiapuram is not in our jurisdiction," said Acahaari.

"I will take ten days' leave and go to Muthiapuram. Whenever I call you or tell you to do something, you apply for shorter leaves, which I will approve. No one should know we're working on this case."

"What will you tell Kulasekaran, sir?" asked Acahaari

"I will tell him I am going to a resort in Tuticorin for meditation and cannot be disturbed," she said with a wink and a smile.

When Prithika arrived in Muthiapuram, she felt as though she had entered heaven. The rains had transformed the village into a lush green paradise. Since she did not want to attract too much attention to herself, she discreetly met Selvi Saroj, the correspondent who had broken Tamini's case on TV in Tuticorin a few days ago, and they arrived at a mutually beneficial agreement.

"I am told the case officer is your boyfriend, and you have excellent local networking. Introduce me to him, and I will ensure you get exclusive scoops on the case," she said. Prithika had done her homework and was aware that the case officer, Arul Iyer, was Selvi's boyfriend.

"Boyfriend or not, you know it will be tough to get a case officer to share information about his case, but I will introduce you to him as my friend. The condition is that you give me regular progress updates, as Arul never shares anything with me," she said.

"Done," said Prithika.

As agreed, Selvi introduced Prithika to Arul as her college friend. Arul had already heard about Prithika, her life journey and her struggle to become a Police Officer and greatly respected her. He shared the case file with her, not because she was Selvi's friend but because Prithika was an excellent investigator, and he also needed help.

According to the case file, Prithika noted that Tamini had died of Cyanide poisoning, and she, too, had a half-read spy novel by her bedside. When they checked the pages, they found that the last page, number 247, had an underlined quote. The quote read, "*The only way to get over the past is to go into eternal sleep.*" Tamini was also sleeping peacefully in her bed, dressed neatly. The crime scene was identical to Jeisy's, except no tea cup was in the sink. Prithika asked Arul to do a toxicology test on the book, and sure enough, traces of Cyanide were found on page 247.

Arul and Prithika reviewed the evidence in both cases and reached on two conclusions. One: The same person committed both murders using the same methodology. Two: The primary suspect was Dr Suryakantam Udayar, now a shift doctor at a local government hospital.

That night, she called Acahaari from a newly bought burner phone as she had switched off her regular phone, pretending to be on a meditation retreat.

"We are dealing with a serial killer. Find out if there is any connection between Tamini and Jeisy," she said.

Then she called Selvi and, as promised, shared the information. The following day, Selvi's evening show was explosive. "The untimely death of teacher Tamini Gounder was tragic, but our channel's investigation reveals a connection between Tamini's murder and the murder of Jeisy Jhonson in Attayampatti three weeks ago. Aside from both victims being of almost similar age and profession, the methodology used to kill both victims is the same: Cyanide poisoning. Both the victims were found sleeping peacefully in bed, and there were no signs of forced entry or a scuffle, which means the killer knew his victims and was there while his victims died."

Inspector Arul Kumar was having dinner when he saw the news. He immediately called Prithika and asked, "Why did you share the information with her? Now the killer will be alerted."

"That is exactly what we want. Now, the killer will panic and make a wrong move. That way, he will be exposed," she replied.

"Where are you now?" asked Arul.

"Following Dr Udayar. He is outside Tamini's house. I want to know what he is up to," she said.

Prithika had been following Dr Udayar for over 24 hours. She noticed he lived alone, cooked and ate alone, and had no friends. Twice, she saw him ride past Tamini's house. Tonight, the full moon was up in the sky. From a distance, she saw Udayar hovering around the house.

As she watched, she saw Udayar break the rear window of Tamini's house, open the kitchen door and enter the house from the back. She followed and confronted him while he was rummaging through her drawers in the living room.

"Put your hands up and step forward, else I will shoot you," she said sternly, catching him unaware from behind.

Dr Udayar whirled around, saw Prithika, and immediately dropped to his knees with his hands held up. "Please don't shoot me. I am no killer," he pleaded.

"What are you doing on a crime scene, then?" asked Prithika, still training her gun on him.

"Looking for the killer," he replied.

"But you are the killer. You killed Jeisy, framed Simran, took a transfer to Muthiapuram and found your second victim. You left Attayampatti the day after Simran was sent to jail," said Prithika.

"No, you got it all wrong. I was ashamed and disgusted with myself for having an affair with someone twenty years younger than me. I met Jeisy at a party, and both of us were drunk, and in a moment of weakness, we made love. I never wanted to have a relationship, but she clung on and kept meeting, calling and texting me till Simran found out. When Jeisy died, I was relieved, but I never knew Simran would get framed for it."

"Framed? All the evidence was against her," said Prithika.

"What evidence? The poor thing went to plead my case with Jeisy and got convicted for her murder," argued Udayar.

"She had Potassium Cyanide powder at home. Her fingerprints were on that book, and she was the last to meet Jeisy," she said.

"Yes, the Cyanide was at our home because I ordered it and asked her to pick it up. It was for the hospital. I was getting late, so I asked her to buy it. I was to take it to the hospital the next day. Her fault was she picked it up for me. Her fingerprints were on the book because she casually picked it up while waiting for Jeisy to make her a cup of tea. Regarding the meeting with Jeisy, I agree she was the last to meet her, but she went there to save our marriage.'

'Look, neither she nor I read spy novels, but as per the media, the books found near the bedside were about espionage in both cases. If she were a criminal, she wouldn't be a fool to leave her fingerprints on the book and her DNA on the teacup for the police. You found a convenient scapegoat in her and pinned everything on her. But I love Simran, and I will prove her innocence,' said Udayar, tears rolling down his cheeks.

After a long silence, Prithika holstered her service revolver and said softly, "I am sorry to have doubted you, Dr Udayar. I am here because even I believe Simran is innocent. Let us not do parallel investigations. Join me in my investigation and share everything you have on the case. Help me arrest the real killer and get Simran out of jail," she requested.

Chapter 5

The next day, Prithika, Dr Udayar, and Arul met in Arul's office. Prithika had briefed Arul about meeting Udayar the previous night.

"I believe the killer was in the room when his victims were dying. He watched Jeisy and Tamini die and then placed them on the bed. He made sure not to leave any fingerprints anywhere. He has to be someone who knows the teachers. He also seems to be a person who knows about forensics, crime, etc, to be able to hide his trail so effectively," said Dr Udayar.

"Hmm... you mean a doctor?" asked Arul sarcastically. He was still suspicious of Dr Udayar.

Udayar rolled his eyes and said, "The way the killer took so much care to arrange the dress nicely and make the victims look peaceful and asleep proves he has OCD. I am a doctor, and I can read symptoms."

"You mean the killer was meticulous like a doctor?" asked Arul, giving Dr Udayar a side glance.

"No, he means the killer has OCD; stop picking on the doctor, Arul," stressed Prithika.

She tapped the photos of the crime scene and said, "The books came from the killer. Looking at the genre, he is clearly a spy novel fan. There are no big bookshops in Attayampatti, and even the ones they have do not have the latest editions, like *The Puppeteer*, which was released recently."

"So?" asked Arul.

"It means the books came from the killer's library, you illiterate," snapped Dr Udayar.

"What kind of books do you have in your house, Dr Udayar?" asked Arul in a menacing tone.

"The genre I like is comedy. Especially about cops who are dimwits," retorted Udayar.

Before Arul could retaliate, Prithika stepped in and changed the topic. "The killer wanted the victims to die on their own. That is why he applied poison to the pages and got them to read the lines on them."

"He could have applied it on the book cover; why on pages 84 and 247?" asked Dr Udayar.

"Because if he had applied on the cover, it would have been detected immediately. He put them on specific pages, made them read, and then when they were dead, he placed the books by the bedside half-open to mislead everyone by making it look like a natural death; a heart attack while sleeping. No one would have expected the Cyanide to be on a specific book page. Gentlemen, we are looking for a brilliant serial killer," said Prithika.

"Some Police officers are brilliant in deduction," said Udayar, taunting Arul.

Smarting under the insult, Arul. "How did the victims know the Cyanide was on those pages?"

"They did not. If I am right, the victims may not even have intended to read the books, as neither were fans of spy novels. So, he made them read it by underlining the sentences on pages 84 and 247. The answer to your question about how he made them do it is simple. He called on them with the books and asked them to read it," said Prithika.

"He came to the victim's house with the book and knocked on their doors. They welcomed him inside, and he gifted them the books. They opened it, and he directed them to read the lines on the pages. They did and died. He lifted them, placed them on the bed, kept the books half open by their bedside and left. What is so difficult to understand?" asked Udayar.

While Arul bristled at the sarcasm, Prithika looked at Jeisy and Tamini's call records. After scrutinising the numbers on their call and received list, she underlined a single number that was present on both the call records. While it appeared only once in Tamini's, the number was recorded several times on Jeisy's call records.

Prithika looked at Arul and said, "This is the number the killer used to keep in touch with the victims. The calls to him were only from Jeisy's number, which means the two corresponded regularly. But in Tamini's case, she only received a single call from the killer."

"The call of death," said Udayar dramatically.

Prithika asked Arul to check the number, though she was sure they could never trace it. "See whose number this is?"

Arul asked his cyber team, who checked and returned with the answer Prithika had expected; "The number is not listed. The caller has used a burner app."

***

Later that night, Acahaari called Prithika and said, "You won't believe what I found out."

"Stop with the suspense and tell me what you found," said Prithika.

"Tamini and Jeisy are related. They are the adopted daughters of SP Suren Pillai, a Malayali police officer living in Ooty. The two escaped a road accident in Ooty when they were two years old. The parents died, but miraculously, the children survived," said Acahaari.

"Do you have the details of their biological parents?" asked Prithika.

"Yes, I have their complete file and history," said Acahaari.

"Send it to me by express courier, along with the address and contact details of SP Suren Pillai."

"I will do that. By the way, Kulasekaran sir is looking frantically for you. He asked me several times about how to contact you, but I said your cell phone was switched off. Give him a call," said Acahaari.

"I will call him once I finish with SP Suren Pillai, I promise," said Prithika.

Aachari's courier arrived the next day. Prithika went through it in great detail, packed her bags, and left for Ooty to meet Pillai. In the meantime, Arul's cyber team traced the IP address of the phone used to call Jeisy and Tamini—a location in Salem. Arul sent the details to Prithika just before her flight took off. She tried to open the message, but the internet wasn't working. She gave up, thinking she would check it once she landed.

***

On the flight to Ooty, Prithika reviewed Aachari's files again and made a note: *"Since the calls came from Jeisy, the probability is that she knew the killer's past and was blackmailing him. So, the killer silenced her first. Tamimi's relation to Jeisy led her to become collateral damage.'* Then, she made a profile of the killer—*A man who has a past which he is trying to hide. A past which is murky enough to bring damage to his present and future. A past that can never come out, even if it means murdering someone. The killer is intelligent enough to plan his kills and courageous enough to carry them through. It is someone who has the experience of killing or seeing people killed.'*

With shivering hands, she wrote a name at the end of the profiling, shut the book, and looked out the window into the setting sun on the horizon as the plane began its descent. When she landed, Prithika called Arul and asked, "You sent me a message, but there was no internet connection; what was it?"

"We got the location from where the calls were made to Tamini and Jeisy," he said. "Where was it from?" asked Prithika.

"From your residence," said Arul.

Prithika felt as though someone had hit her on her chest with a sledgehammer. She took a deep breath and said softly, "I will call you back."

Then, she switched off the burner phone she had used the entire time she was out of the office, switched on her official phone for the first time in seven days, and checked the call directory. There was one call from her father and twenty-seven missed calls from Kulasekaran. She dialled Kulasekaran and waited.

"Where the hell are you?" asked Kulasekaran in anger. Then he softened his tone and said gently, "We received an anonymous message with multiple proofs that Jeisy's killer is not Simran but someone else."

"Is it my father?" asked Prithika calmly.

"Yes. We have taken Ayyaswamy into custody, but he refuses to answer our questions. He says he wants to speak to you first. He has been in custody for 24 hours now, and I have been trying to contact you desperately, but your phone was switched off. I need you to come back immediately," said Kulasekaran.

"Sure, sir," said Prithika, her eyes brimming with tears.

Chapter 6

SP Suren Pillai looked sad and lonely, but he greeted Prithika with warmth and respect. "I have heard about you. Thank you for finding Jeisy's killer. I wish you all the best in solving Tamini's case, too," he said, handing her a cup of hot coffee.

"I am sorry to disappoint you, but Simran was not Jeisy's killer," she said, accepting the coffee.

"Then who is?" asked Pillai

"Well, I am here to meet you regarding that," she said softly as she handed him the two files Acahaari had sent of the biological parents of Tamini and Jeisy.

"Tell me everything about them, please," she said, looking at Pillai.

"Jeisy and Tamini are daughters of two Police officers who trained under me as cadets. I was the head of the training academy in Ooty then. Unfortunately, both their parents died in a car crash when they were just two years old. The children survived miraculously. When the Police informed me and told me that none of their relatives were responding to the calls and no one was willing to take responsibility for the children, I spoke to my wife, and together, we decided to adopt them. We never had children of our own, so it was a blessing in disguise for us."

"How did their parents die?"

"The brakes of their jeep failed while returning from a late-night Police function. The jeep they were travelling in went over the cliff but got stuck on a tree branch. The parents, who were not wearing seatbelts, fell into the gorge and died. The children were strapped to the centre of the back seat, so they survived."

"Why are both your adopted daughters English teachers?" asked Prithika.

"My wife was an English teacher in a government school in Ooty. She encouraged them to become teachers, too."

"Where is your wife now?"

"She is no more. She died of lung cancer several years ago," said Pillai.

He sighed and looked at a picture of Tamini and Jeisy on the mantle. "Tamini had chosen not to marry and was looking for a transfer to Ooty to be with me. Jeisy told me she had found someone, but he was married. I told her not to ruin a family for her happiness. I invited them both to Ooty, and they were to come home this summer holidays. But fate had something else in store for me. First, I lost my wife and now my children." Pillai started sobbing.

Prithika consoled him and said, "One final question." She showed him a photograph and asked, "Do you know him?"

Pillai nodded as he wiped his eyes. "Yes. He trained under me as well," he said.

They spoke at length for another hour, and finally, Prithika left. As she got into her taxi, she held his hand and said, "I am an Aravani, but if you accept me, I could be your daughter as long as you live."

Pillai hugged Prithika tightly and whispered, "Thank you, my daughter."

Chapter 7

Prithika sat before DSP Kulasekaran as he explained Ayyaswamy's arrest. "I know this is painful, but your father insists on not speaking to anyone but you, so please question him and get him to confess," said Kulasekaran.

"What is the evidence against him?" asked Prithika.

Kulasekaran pushed a file in front of her and said, "Both the books found on the crime scene are from Ayyaswamy's library. We found the driver who drove him three days before the murder to Muthiapuram and back. His name is Doraiswamy and his picture is in the file. When constable John searched your house, he found a bottle of Potassium Cyanide powder and a burner phone with Ayyaswamy's fingerprints in your storeroom. Also, the number tallies with his calls to Jeisy and Tamini. It is an open-and-shut case. All we need is his confession, and you can close this case."

Prithika picked up the folder and stood up. "What was Ayyaswamy's motive?" she asked Kulasekaran.

"We don't know. I hope he will talk to you and confess," said Kulasekaran.

"Until we establish motive, he is only an accused, and until then, this is not an open-and-shut case," said Prithika, looking directly at Kulasekaran.

Prithika saw anger in Kulasekaran's eyes for a split second, but then he mellowed immediately. "Yes, you are right. It was my mistake to jump to conclusions. This is your case; go solve it." Kulasekaran patted Prithika on the shoulder and sent her on her way.

As Prithika left Kulasekaran's office, she texted Acahaari a picture and said, "Go to the driver and question him about driving my father to Muthiapuram and back. Ask him the way you do and get the truth."

Then she went straight to the holding cell where Ayyaswami was being held. She asked the constable to open the door and went in. As soon as Ayyaswamy saw Prithika, he broke down. "I am so sorry, my child. They say I am the killer. I have no clue how all this evidence is piling up against me. I don't mind what they do to me, but I don't want to become the reason for your loss of reputation," he cried.

"Forget my reputation; just answer my questions directly. Did you kill Jeisy?"

"No. Why would I…" Prithika cut off Ayyaswamy.

"Stick to the point. How did the books disappear from your house?"

"I don't know. I noticed they were missing when constable John came to question me. He asked me if the books belonged to me and I said yes. He asked me for them and when I searched the bookshelf, they were not there," he said.

"What was Potassium Cyanide powder doing in our house?" she asked.

"I don't know. I have never bought Cyanide in my life. Constable John told me he found a bottle in our store room at the back. I hardly go there. When I told him I didn't know about the bottle, he asked me to look at it carefully before denying it. I did and insisted I had not bought it. The same was the case with the cell phone.

he showed me that also and said they found it in the store room." Ayyaswami was in tears.

"Did you touch the bottle and the phone?" asked Prithika.

"Yes, I did when John showed them to me and asked me to check if they were mine," he said.

"Did you go to Muthiapuram?" she asked.

"Yes, I did."

"Why?"

"There has been no postmaster in Muthiapuram for a year now. I got a call from the postal department asking if I would like to take charge there. Since retirement, I have been doing nothing except for sitting and watching TV. It was a three-year contract, and the salary was good, so I said I would do it after I saw the place. So I went there for a recce," said Ayyaswamy.

"And what have you decided?" asked Prithika.

"There is nothing to decide. They already have a postmaster. Someone played a prank on me, I think. I called you when I was in Muthiapuram, but your phone was coming 'switched off'," he said.

Prithika looked at her phone and saw an old missed call from her father, which she had ignored to respond. She smiled for the first time, hugged him and said, "You may have to spend one more night here, Father, and then I will come to fetch you."

By the time Prithika left Ayyaswamy's cell, it was late evening. She met DSP Kulasekaran and told him she needed to question Ayyaswami again in the morning before she reported her findings. Kulasekaran agreed and left for the day.

After leaving the Police Station, she called Acahaari and said, "I have sent you a picture. After you are finished with the driver, go to the old Shiva temple, meet the Pujari and ask him if he recognises the picture I sent you."

At around 9:30 pm, Acahaari called. He was sixteen kilometres away at the temple. He had finished interrogating the driver and had talked to the Pujari as well.

"The driver confessed," he said.

"Did you do the third degree on him?" asked Prithika

"No, ma'am. I am a peace-loving person. I showed the driver three packets of Heroine in his dicky and told him he could kiss his family life goodbye. He sang like a canary."

"You know using items from the evidence room is illegal?" asked Prithika.

"I know. The Heroine will be back on the shelf tonight." Prithika could sense the laugh in his voice. She sighed and said, "All is fair in love and war. What did the Pujari say?"

"He recognised the face. I am still with him and he says he wants to speak with you." Acahaari handed over the phone to the Pujari.

"Are you Prithika?" asked the Pujari.

"Yes, Baba," she said.

"Nice to hear your voice after such a long time. The last I heard was when you cried as a baby," said the Pujari. The two spoke for a few more minutes, and then the Pujari returned the phone to Acahaari.

"What do you want me to do? Acahaari asked Prithika.

After a profound silence, Prithika said to Acahaari, "Nothing. Go home and rest. I will meet you directly at Kulasekaran sir's residence tomorrow morning for the briefing. Be there by 9:00 a.m. I will come after meeting my father in his cell at 8:00 am," she disconnected.

Chapter 8

When Prithika arrived at Kulasekaran's residence for the morning briefing, he insisted she have breakfast with him. They sat at the dining table, he at the head of the table and she to his right.

"It is your favourite, idli and chicken stew," said Kulasekaran, serving her two idlis and a small bowl of stew.

As they ate, Prithika asked Kulasekaran, "How did you know I like idli and stew?"

"Ayyaswami told me. Those meetings with your dad were spent discussing you most of the time. I took away a lot of information about you during those meetings," said Kulasekaran with a mischievous smile.

"How did the books leave my house?" asked Prithika with a smile as she finished eating the idlis.

"I don't know. I assume Ayyaswamy carried it with him when he met his victims." said Kulasekaran as he put another idli on her plate.

"How are you so convinced that my father killed the two teachers?" she asked.

"I told you, Dorai the driver came to the Police station and told Constable John that he saw the news about Tamini and Jeisy's murders being similar and remembered that he had carried your father to Muthiapuram a day before the murder. I remembered you telling me that he loved reading and had a decent library in his room, so I asked John to search for the two books. They were missing. Then I gave the order for the house search, and we found the phone and the Cyanide with his prints on it."

Prithika washed her hands in a washbasin beside the dining room, and walked to the living room.

Kulasekaran followed her with a mug of coffee. He walked to the sofa and sat down. Prithika followed him and sat opposite him. Behind him, she could see Acahaari, who had arrived by then, standing in the doorway.

She looked at Kulasekaran and said, "With your permission, I want to tell a story before we talk about Ayyaswami, sir."

"Sure, go ahead," said Kulasekaran, sipping his coffee.

Prithika started her narration. "This is the story of a young, innocent baby born more than three decades ago into a family in Ooty. When the father discovered his child was an Aravani, he was livid and asked his wife to get rid of the infant. The wife refused. A month later, the father got rid of the child on a visit to Attayampatti to meet his in-laws, Without the mother's knowledge on a rainy morning, he abandoned the thirty-day-old infant in a Shiva temple in Attayampatti and returned home.

When the mother came to know what her husband had done, she was heartbroken. While the father told the world that they had lost their beautiful child to an incurable disease, the guilt-ridden mother, terrified of her husband, confessed to her two friends and committed suicide. Unfortunately for the father, the two friends turned out to be none other than his two friends' wives. Though the father managed to convert the suicide into a normal death, the friends, along with their husbands, confronted the cruel father at a function and asked him to confess to the Police, or they would turn him in. The cunning father agreed to admit and, while leaving the function, removed the brakes from the jeep the friends had come in. As the friends and their wives with their two babies were returning home that night, the brakes of their jeep failed, and they went over the cliff into a Gorge. But look at fate. The two children survived and were adopted by their Police training head. In the meantime, back in Attayampatti, the Pujari handed over the Aravani child to a sterile postman, who raised her as his daughter. All three children grew up. Inspired by their adopted mother, the training head's children, Jeisy and Tamini, became English teachers—one in Attayampatti government school and the other in Muthiapuram government school. The third child, the one adopted by the Postman, became Prithika, a Police Officer.'

"How is all this connected with the two murders, Prithika?" asked Kulasekaran.

"It is connected, sir, but have some patience. The story will reveal all the connections soon," she said.

"Go ahead," said Kulasekaran.

"Three decades later, one of the teachers, Jeisy Jhonson, found the letter written by Prithika's mother to her mother. She found it in a box in the attic that had come as part of the items from her parent's house after the adoption. It revealed the story of the grief-stricken mother and how she lost her only child. It talked about the cruel father who abandoned the infant on the steps of a temple and how she was going to commit suicide."

Prithika looked at Kulasekaran and asked, "Does the story ring a bell, sir?"

"Why should it ring a bell?" asked Kulasekaran.

"Because the cruel father is none other than you, DSP Kulasekaran. I am your daughter, and you left me on the temple steps that day because you could not bear the shame of being a father to an Aravani. You threatened my mother, and she committed suicide out of guilt and grief. You murdered your batch mates and their wives when they confronted you with the truth because you wanted to hide your dirty secret."

"Three decades later, you came to know about me, and you had a change of heart. You wanted to be close to me, so you took a transfer to Attayampatti. But just when you thought we had started bonding, Jeisy called and blackmailed you. You decided that humouring her instead of confronting her was best as you were planning her murder on the side. When you saw the library in Ayyaswamy's house, an idea came to mind. You thought of plans A and B in case you needed a fallback. Your plan A was to kill Jeisy and pass it off as a natural death. It failed when I suspected it was a murder. But then you had your Plan B ready to frame Ayyaswamy. Unfortunately, innocent Simran entered the plot unknowingly and got convicted. You breathed a sigh of relief for a while, but then, being a police officer, you had to ensure no leads were left behind. So, you checked to see if Jeisy had shared my mother's letter with anyone and to your surprise, you found she had sent a scanned copy to Tamini. So, you approached Tamini, saying you are her father's friend, and murdered her too. You wanted to destroy the evidence but could not find her laptop. You were busy locating her computer when I went on leave. When you saw the news about both murders being linked, you knew I was on the case, but you could not contact me. In my absence, you resorted to Plan B and framed Ayyaswamy."

"This is all a figment of your imagination," said Kulasekaran, but Prithika could see beads of sweat on his forehead.

"The Pujari at the Shiva temple identified you as the father who abandoned his daughter on the temple steps. Dorai confessed that, he made the call to my father, pretending to be from the postal department on your instructions. He also admitted that he returned with my father the day after the murder as instructed by you. My father made the mistake of staying the night of the murder in Muthiapuram, hoping to meet me, but he got saved, as he called me that night. A killer would never announce his presence in a crime scene, especially to his daughter. Unable to contact me, he left the next day."

"To frame my father, you told your loyal and trusted partner in crime, John to search my house, plant the Cyanide and the burner phone. John ensured my father touched both and got his fingerprints. You were guaranteed a watertight case but forgot I am your daughter, and I, too, have the same cunning mind."

"What gave it away?" asked Kulasekaran, who looked tired and drained as he realised the game was up.

"The cleanliness of the murder site. I have watched you long enough to know you have OCD. After putting the victims to bed, you made the mistake of arranging their dress neatly around them. The scene looked clinically clean. I saw Simran's house when she was in jail and how unkept it was; that is when I felt I had made a mistake. But then I saw no motive in you killing her, so I dropped it. Jeisy and Tamini's relationship helped a lot, and when I met with Pillai, I checked Tamini's laptop. The letter was in her junk folder, as Jeisy had sent the mail from a newly created email address. That letter closed the loop. My only objective was to remove my father's name from the mess. Interrogating Dorai and John completed that. John confessed to planting the evidence when I told him an abandoned CCTV camera in the store had recorded everything."

"Was there a CCTV camera in the store?" asked Kulasekaran

"No. I lied," she said with a smile.

"I did all this to be with you. I was planning to tell you that I am your father. I took a transfer to be with you, my child." Kulasekaran said.

"And how were you planning to hide the past? By killing Ayyaswamy in jail? By murdering the Pujari and Mr Pillai?" asked Prithika.

"No, that is not true," Kulasekaran pleaded.

"John told us everything in his confession. You say you did all this to be with me, but I think you did this to hide your past. I was just an excuse. Admit it, Father; you are nothing but a cold-hearted murderer who killed his wife, friends, and their families. You tasted blood, and now you were planning to kill three more innocent people," said Prithika.

"What now?" asked Kulasekaran as he walked towards a side table with an unlit cigarette in his mouth. Aachari thought Kulasekaran was opening the drawer for a lighter, but Prithika read Kulasekaran's mind.

"Now? Well, I arrest you, take your confession and put you behind bars for life," said Prithika, watching Kulasekaran's right hand as he opened the drawer.

Kulasekaran opened the drawer, removed his service revolver and swirled around to fire at Prithika, but she had anticipated it. She dived to her right with her revolver in her hand. As she landed on the floor, she aimed and fired. The bullet hit him in the stomach, and he stumbled backwards. By then, Aachari realised what was happening, and he, too, fired. His bullet hit Kulasekaran in the back, and he fell face forward. The revolver skidded away from him.

Prithika picked up Kulasekaran's revolver and checked the cylinder to remove the bullets, but it was empty. She walked up to the bleeding DSP, turned him and put his head on her lap. She looked at him, "Your revolver had no bullets. Why did you do it?"

"Better to die at the hands of my daughter than rot in jail. With my death, your name will shine in the annals of the police force. What I could not give you when I was alive, I give you with my death. Forgive me, my child; I am your sinner."

Kulasekaran raised his hand one last time, caressing Prithika's cheek and whispered, "God bless you, Shakti." Then, with a long sigh, Kulasekaran died.

Prithika closed Kulasekaran's eyes, got up and left the room. As she left the house, she opened her notebook and looked at the name she had scribbled on her flight to Ooty. At the bottom of her notes was the name *DSP Kulasekaran.* She scratched out the name and threw the book into a dustbin.

***

Epilogue

A few months later….

Inspector Prithika was reading a file in her office when she got a call from the IGP in HO. "Good morning, sir," she said, standing up.

"The CBI chief wanted a person in Salem, and I recommended your name. Come and collect your letter tomorrow from me," said the IGP.

The next day, when she arrived at the IGP's office and took her letter, she saw her name written as 'Shakti'. "Why is my name mentioned as Shakti, sir?" she asked.

"That is the code name assigned to you by CBI."

Zidd

Inspired by the story of a child ghost at the Lothian Cemetery in New Delhi, this gripping psychological thriller delves into the chilling tale of a Delhi family besieged by a terrifying paranormal invasion.

Prologue

Post-partition, in 1947, the newly formed Indian government took over all the land and properties vacated by those who had left for Pakistan. It auctioned them to the highest bidders who had stayed in India. Ram Prakash Rastogi, a wealthy garments merchant, was one such recipient of a beautiful bungalow called Mirza Manzil. Despite the house being half-burnt in the riots, he saw its potential. With unwavering determination, he refurbished it and renamed it "Rastogi Mansion," transforming the British-era bungalow into a work of art.

The spacious two-story bungalow with an internal wrap-around balcony overlooked a central courtyard, which received sunlight from a central atrium, which was open to the skies. The entire property sat on a two-acre, well-manicured green plot in Mehrauli, on the outskirts of Delhi. The bungalow was built on 5,000 sq ft of land; the rest was an open lawn with fruit trees and flowering bushes.

The love for music, art, and literature was deeply ingrained in the Rastogi family. When Ram Prakash bought the Rastogi Mansion, the first thing he did was to convert the large basement into a beautiful library. The shelves were filled with thousands of books, of which half were poems written by the best poets worldwide. Ram's favourites were the Urdu and Hindi poetry written by renowned Indian and Persian poets. Every day after returning from his garments shop, he would do his prayers, settle down in his red velvet armchair, and read poetry for hours until his wife called him for dinner. Ram Prakash had one son, Omprakash Rastogi. So he left everything to Om when he died. After Ram's demise, Om, a carbon copy of Ram, followed the same ritual.

Chapter 1

Om Prakash had two sons. Vijay Rastogi, the 45-year-old eldest son and the inheritor of the family garment business in Chandni Chowk, continued his father and grandfather's love for poetry as he himself was a poet, writing in Hindi and Urdu. Like his predecessors, Vijay would also return from the garment shop and immerse himself in the library, reading rare Hindi and Urdu books on poetry he regularly sourced from around the world.

Om Prakash would celebrate this rich literary heritage and host an annual mushaira function in the library, a day after Shivratri every year. This vibrant event served as a platform for poets and shayars from across India to unite, fostering a lively atmosphere of shared love for the literary arts. For Vijay, it was an opportunity to showcase his poems, and for the family, it was a chance to honour their deep-rooted literary legacy.

Vijay's other love was his school and college mate, a beautiful Brahmin girl from Lucknow named Seema Kashyap. While Vijay ran the garment business, Seema, a year younger than him, completed her medical studies and became a paediatric Surgeon. The two of them were deeply in love and had planned to get married, but Seema's father, who never approved of Vijay, got her married to a doctor from Kanpur. After the wedding, Seema relocated to Kanpur with her husband, leaving a heartbroken Vijay in Mehrauli.

After three years of marriage, Seema, who could never get over Vijay, rebelled against her father, divorced her husband, and returned to Mehrauli. Unfortunately for her, Vijay had lost faith in women and chose to remain a bachelor all his life. Though he did not welcome her back, deep inside, he still had feelings for her. A complex personality, Vijay spent his entire day at the garment shop and the evenings in his basement library. While he chose to remain single, deep inside, he hoped they would reunite one day. In the meantime, Seema joined a local hospital two kilometres from the Rastogi Mansion. She had decided that either she would marry Vijay or lead a spinster's life.

The younger son, Ajay Rastogi, 38, was an outgoing social character with many friends. After completing his engineering degree at IIT Kanpur, he moved to London as an engineering consultant for a large MNC. A few years later, he fell in love with an English nurse named Grace Jones and married her against Om's wishes. Grace was the only child of David Jones, a single parent and civil lawyer who helped Ajay in getting his British citizenship quickly. A year later, tragedy struck the couple—David died of cancer and Ajay lost his mother. She was heartbroken with his decision to marry a Christian and settle in the UK. When Ajay wanted to come for her funeral, a livid Om sent word through Vijay that the Rastogis had cut off all relations with him.

Years passed. One day, 80-year-old Om received a message and some pictures from Grace on his WhatsApp. The message read, *"Congratulations, you have become a grandpa."* The pictures were of his newborn grandson. An excited Om called Grace impulsively and asked her, "What have you named him?"

"Adit," she replied.

Om's joy knew no bounds. It was the name he had thought of for Ajay when he was born, but later, it was changed to please his wife. Grace's gesture touched Om's heart and dissolved the hate he harboured for Ajay. After a long conversation with Grace, he wholeheartedly accepted her as his daughter-in-law and asked her to come and visit him.

After Adit's birth, Ajay left his job and started his own business, which did well for five years. However, when the UK economy tanked, his company also dwindled and soon became bankrupt. Unable to look after his family, he sent Grace and Adit to India to be with Om and, a few months later, followed them to India. An empathetic and understanding Om welcomed Ajay and his family with open arms.

One night, after a family dinner, Om and Vijay were cleaning the small Shiva temple that Vijay had built in the far-right corner of the family compound when Om asked Vijay, "How long will you hold a grudge, Vijay?

"What are you talking about?" Vijay asked.

"Seema divorced her husband to be with you, but you rejected her. Yet she chose to remain single and wait for your call. I think the time has come for you to forget, forgive and move on."

"Let me think about it," Vijay replied. Vijay's response gave Om some hope. He realised that Vijay was not opposed to the suggestion.

Chapter 2

Three weeks had passed since Ajay and his family arrived, and Grace and Adit had settled well into their new home. Both were crazy about Indian food, so Raju Kaka, the cook and caretaker of Rastogi Mansion, was their favourite as he made various local delicacies for them.

Despite being a foreigner, Grace made some local friends and even had one of them as her Hindi tutor. Enterprising and bubbly, Grace soon got a job at the British embassy as the embassy clinic assistant, and six-year-old Adit was admitted into an excellent local school. Ajay used Om's car to drop Grace and Adit off every morning at their respective destination and pick them up at 3:00 p.m.

One day, after Vijay had left for the garment shop—Grace and Adit dropped off at work and school—Ajay was sitting at home watching television. Om asked him, "Thankfully, Grace and Adit have settled well. Tell me, what have you planned for your future?"

"I need to start earning, I guess," said Ajay.

"Why don't you join Vijay in the garments business? It is doing well."

"I don't want to sell underwear and bras like Bhaiyya, Baba. I want to start a new-age business where I don't have to worry about manufacturing, logistics, sales, etc. I want to be more like a trader, where you get a ready product from one, sell it to another, and make a commission. I was doing that in London, and I am good at it.

However, the difficulty in this country is that, as a British citizen, if I want to start a business, I need to either have an Indian partner or give up my British passport, and I have no intentions of the latter," said Ajay continuing to look at the TV.

Then he turned towards Om and said precisely what Om had feared he would say. "The garments business belongs to me as well. Tell Bhaiyya to do a valuation and give me my share. I will find a local partner and set up my business." Though saddened by Ajay's demand, Om discussed it with Vijay later that night to ask his view on this.

"Baba, if we sell the business and split it, the money won't be enough for him to set up any business. We best sell the business and give him the entire amount. If his business runs well, then Grace may not need to work. You are getting old and need someone with you all the time. Grace is a qualified nurse. She can look after you," said Vijay.

Om looked at his generous and empathetic son and said softly, "You are like your mother. She also used to find joy in giving. You gave away Seema for her father's happiness, sacrificed a married life to look after me, and now you are giving up the business for Ajay and his family. You are my Ram. But even Ram has to survive; what will you do for a living?"

"He can work in the embassy, Baba," said Grace, who had overheard everything.

"What do you mean?" asked Om.

"Vijay is an engineer with an MBA. The embassy has an opening for an administrative head—someone with management experience and technical skills. Vijay Bhaiyya fits all the criteria, and the salary is excellent."

"What are the working hours?" asked Vijay

"It is from 6 a.m. to 10 p.m., but the HOD has to be there from 6 a.m. to 2 p.m. as they have a number two to cover from 2 p.m. to 10 p.m. The embassy closes after that. If Bhaiyya gets selected, he will have a handsome salary, and we can work and commute together," said Grace with a big smile.

"And Ajay can focus on his business without worrying about Grace and Adit," added Om.

"And I will have enough time to focus on my poetry too," said Vijay, beaming from ear to ear.

"And Vijay baba can think of getting married also," said Raju Kaka while entering with hot Pakoras and tea for everyone. Then he looked at Om and said, "It looks like God has found a solution to all your problems,"

When Ajay joined them for tea, Om briefed him about the plan. An overwhelmed Ajay hugged Vijay and whispered, "I will never forget this generosity."

Vijay hugged him back tightly and whispered, "Other than my Shiva Mandir, everything else is yours, brother,"

Two weeks later, there were two good pieces of news, but the third was not so good. The good news was that one of Om's business friends and competitors had decided to buy the garments business for a good price, and Vijay had got the job in the British embassy as the Head of Administration. The third—about Ajay's local partner worried Om and Vijay—Ajay had chosen to partner with a gentleman called Abhinav Banerjee, a local businessman who owned an imported car's showroom.

"The man does not have a good reputation. He is alcoholic, a gambler and a womaniser. There is a rumour that he murdered his wife," said Om.

"This is the problem in India. Everything is hearsay and we believe it. No wonder this country is still backward. I am not bothered by what he does in his private space and time. He has a trading business that I am interested in, and I feel if we invest more money in marketing and acquiring more cars, we will make a very good profit," said Ajay.

Om was about to argue when Vijay intervened and said, "Ajay is a grown-up man who has run a business in the UK, Babuji. He knows better. Let it be." He turned to Ajay and said, "Wish you all the best brother."

Ajay did not miss Grace's worried look or Vijay's comforting nod to her. Later in the evening, Vijay took everyone out to dinner and a movie to lighten the mood.

***

Chapter 3

With Ajay busy with his business plans, Vijay, Grace, and Adit became very close. Every day Vijay, Grace and Adit would leave together. After dropping Adit at school, the two of them would go to work together. In the evenings, Vijay would play with Adit and as sundown approached, retire to his library to write poetry. After his bath, Adit would also join him there. Soon, the two formed a routine—every evening, Vijay would wait for Adit's arrival. The moment the clock would hit 7:00 p.m., there would be a knock on the library door, followed by a sweet voice asking, "Uncle, can I come".

Vijay would reply, *"Aaiye Chote Nawab, aaiye."* Then, while Vijay returned to his writing table to continue writing his poetry, Adit would browse through books and finally settle down in Ram Prakash's favourite red velvet armchair with a book from the library. After each stanza, Vijay would recite loudly and wait for Adit's compliments. Most days, Adit slept with Vijay until Ajay came home, after which Grace would carry him back to their bedroom. As time passed, Vijay and Adit started bonding very well. Adit loved listening to Vijay, and Vijay enjoyed having Adit as his audience.

In the meantime, Grace and Om also grew close. The two would sit and chat on the large green lawns of the compound every evening as they waited for Ajay to return from his drinking spree with his newly found partner. Grace was worried about Ajay's growing alcoholism. Most evenings, to keep her mind away from her worries, Om would educate her on everything about their family. From these conversations, she learned about Vijay and Seema's story.

"Why don't you take the initiative and chat with Seema? If she is willing, you can broach the topic with Vijay," Grace advised.

As months rolled by, the rest of the inhabitants in the house became very close to each other, except Ajay, who spent most of his time with Abhinav and his girlfriends in various clubs under the pretext of business. Most days, he would come home drunk and late. Om and Grace would try speaking to him, but an intoxicated Ajay would hardly listen. Trusting Abhinav more than his family, one day, he told Abhinav about his deteriorating relationship with Grace. Instead of helping him, Abhinav further poisoned his mind by telling him lies about Vijay and Grace. "They come and go together, shop and eat together, and your son treats him like a father. Better check if your wife is treating him as her husband." Abhinav instigated.

As days passed, Ajay's drinking got worse, and with Abhinav regularly poisoning his mind, there were regular fights between him and Grace. Additionally, a scared Adit refused to leave Vijay's side and stayed away from Ajay. This irritated him further.

One night, when Ajay came home drunk and started abusing Grace, Om tried to stop him, but Ajay pushed him off and went to hit Grace. Vijay, who had heard the commotion, came running down. When he saw Ajay raising his hand at Grace, he stepped in, slapped him, and told him to behave himself. Humiliated in front of everyone, a drunk Ajay retorted, "Abhinav was right. You two *are* sleeping together."

Hearing this, Om lost control and ordered Ajay to leave his house, but Vijay intervened and stopped him by saying it was not Ajay but the alcohol he had consumed that was speaking. A livid Ajay stumbled back into his bedroom, but not before threatening Vijay, "You ruined my family; see what I will do to you."

After everyone had fallen asleep, Vijay searched for Abhinav and found him in a club with his girlfriends. He confronted him and accused him of poisoning Ajay's mind. When Abhinav told him to get lost, Vijay got angry and slapped him. Soon, a fight ensued, and Vijay thrashed Abhinav badly.

The following morning, Ajay flew into a rage when he learned about the fight and that Abhinav was hospitalised. He told Abhinav that he would file an FIR against Vijay, but Abhinav counselled him not to lose his temper. "Don't do anything for a week. Let them feel everything has died independently, and then make your move. If you must ruin Vijay, then you must move strategically."

"What is your plan?" asked Ajay.

"To start with, ask for the land surrounding the house. Tell your father that Vijay can keep the house, and you need the land to open up a new showroom and set up your office. This way, you would have surrounded him. Then, we will harass him daily, so much that he will be forced to leave the house. He has already lost the business; he will be ruined with no land or house. That is the best way to get back," advised Abhinav.

Ajay was thrilled with the idea and laid low for a week. Everyone soon forgot about the incident, and life moved on. With Grace busy at her work as she had started doing double shifts due to work demands, Vijay took charge of Adit's studies and helped him with homework and assignments after work. Om spent time with his senior citizen friends in the morning and read poetry in the afternoons. He also started talking to Seema separately without Vijay's knowledge and soon re-established a relationship. They started meeting occasionally at the market and discussed a future with Vijay. Seema was happy that Om was taking the initiative to reunite them.

***

The following Sunday, while everyone was having breakfast, Ajay demanded the partition of the property from Om. "I want to expand my business; hence, I need land for a large showroom. Let Vijay Bhaiyya keep the house. You write off the land to me. With the showroom next door, Grace, Adit, and I will also be there to look after you," he said.

"The government plans to build a state highway over our land. If not tomorrow, they will come for that land one day, and you will have to sell it to them. What will you do then?" asked Om.

"Who told you about this?" asked Ajay

"Mr Jitendra Agarwal, the director of MCD, is my friend and he warned me," replied Om.

"If that is the issue, then I will risk it. I will cross that bridge when I come to it. You give me the land." Ajay demanded.

"Since you came, all you have been doing is partitioning everything I have. Why are you so hell-bent on breaking this family?" shouted Om.

"You have earned none of this. Everything you are enjoying has been given to you by Grandpa, so don't teach me morals and values." Ajay shouted back.

Vijay intervened and said softly, "If he is so insistent about having it, give him the land, Baba. I don't need it." Then he looked at Ajay and asked sarcastically, "Can you at least leave the Shiv Mandir for the family?"

"No. I don't believe in religion," snapped Ajay.

Seeing Grace's astonishment, Vijay gave her a comforting nod and asked Adit sweetly, "Will you help Chacha shift the deity and the other items in the temple to the library, nawab?"

A frightened Adit nodded as he moved closer to Vijay. As Ajay got up to leave, Vijay said, "It is Adit's birthday today, and we have organised a party at 4:00 p.m., so please come home on time."

"I know," Ajay lied. Then he looked at Adit and said, "When I come home, I will bring you a lovely gift." Ajay left without even wishing his son a happy birthday.

After he left, Vijay and Om met with their lawyer and asked him to prepare the land transfer documents.

In the evening, everyone waited for Ajay to cut the cake, but when he did not come or answer his phone, they celebrated Adit's birthday. Ajay came home drunk at night with a red toy train for Adit and started calling out to him. When Vijay told him that Adit was asleep as he had school the next day, Ajay insisted on seeing Adit. He went to Vijay's room, woke the sleeping child, and gave him the toy. A scared and angry Adit threw the train without even looking at it. This angered Ajay, and he slapped Adit. When Adit started crying, Vijay could not control himself, so he punched Ajay and knocked him out cold.

Chapter 4

Hurt and humiliated, Ajay packed his bags and moved into a hotel the next day. He also hired a civil contractor to commence the land excavation, before it was transferred to his name.

Two days later, when the lawyer handed over the land papers to Ajay, he and Abhinav rejoiced. Three days later, as the rest of the family watched, Ajay and Abhinav organised the Bhoomi Poojan ceremony. After the pooja, Ajay ordered the contractor to break ground. As the blades of the earth mover hit the green soil, they dug deep and pulled out the first lump of soil. While Ajay and Abhinav clapped in joy, Om, who had Adit on his lap and Grace and Vijay beside him, watched his father's land being destroyed. Sitting on his grandpa's lap Adit, watched the earth mover dig. Then suddenly, without a warning, he jumped out of Om's lap and raced towards the earth mover.

"Stop, Adit, stop," Om shouted.

"Adit, wait," Grace screamed.

"Stop the digging, stop the digging," Vijay ordered as he raced towards Adit. But Ajay, who was also racing towards the earth mover, reached him first. Adit, who had already reached the mud pile, put his hand in it and pulled out a yellow object. Even as he looked at the object, Ajay reached him and slapped him hard. "You bloody dumb child; you could have got killed, and I would have been in jail. Go back to your mother," he pushed Adit rudely towards Vijay and then shouted at Om. "If you can't handle him, why do you carry him everywhere you go?"

Vijay grabbed Adit, walked up to Ajay, held him by his collar, and said, "Don't you dare hit Adit. Also, remember, you would have been nothing but a jobless shithead if Babuji had not given you money and this land. The next time you think of shouting at him, keep this in mind," he said as he pushed Ajay, who stumbled backwards and fell on the wet pile of dug up soil. Then he looked at Adit and asked sternly, "Why did you run?"

Adit looked at Vijay and held out the object. It was a yellow-coloured toy bus. He looked at it lovingly and said softly, "I found my bus." Seeing the innocent look on Adit's face, Vijay's eyes moistened. He hugged Adit tightly and walked towards the house.

Abhinav looked at an embarrassed Ajay and said, "Hope now you know what status you have in your house. They think you are a shithead. Are you going to sit quietly or retaliate?"

"I will show them what I can do," growled Ajay as he got up. Then he looked at the machine operator and said, "Break that bloody Shiva temple," The earth mover moved towards the temple and with one stroke, brought it down. The demolition was so hard that it broke the stone deity as well.

Back in the house, Vijay controlled his grief for the broken temple and deity and pacified a frightened Adit. "Here, give me the toy. I will wash and dry it for you, then you can play with it all day." He said as he walked towards the washroom.

When Vijay handed him a clean toy bus, Adit smiled and said, "Thank you, Chachu. You are the best!" Seeing the joy on his face, Vijay hugged him tightly and whispered, "I will always be there for you son."

***

Weeks passed. While Grace and Vijay got busy with work, Ajay was unhappy because three contractors had deserted him halfway through the job, and his excavation had hardly moved. It was as though a bad omen had befallen the project. Since he had given the power of attorney to Abhinav, he had to go through him for everything, and Abhinav was with his girlfriends all the time.

After the incident, Adit went completely quiet. Every day, after school. He would sit alone in his room or the library and play with the toy bus. When he got bored with the toy, he would place it on the carrier of his tricycle and ride all around the building. He started sleeping alone in his room on the first floor and studying independently. With Adit becoming increasingly aloof, a worried Vijay decided to show him to Dr Ratnakar, a child Psychologist and also his friend.

Dr Ratnakar worked in the same hospital as Seema. When Om learned that an appointment had been fixed for the week after, he felt this was an opportunity to get Seema and Vijay together. So, he called Seema and asked if she could accompany Vijay and Adit. "Since you are a Paediatric Surgeon in the same hospital, you would be better suited to talk to Dr Ratnakar and understand the real issue," he said.

Seema agreed and said she would come home on the day of the appointment to accompany Vijay and Adit.

In the meantime, the excavation work continued to drag under a fourth contractor. To add to his misery, Ajay found that the money in his bank account was depleting. On questioning Abhinav about the same, he got a reply that the money was being used to order new cars. Though Abhinav showed him some documents, Ajay suspected he was siphoning money from the account. Unable to gather the courage to confront Abhinav or solve the contractor issue, a frustrated Ajay found refuge in alcohol. Despite repeated requests from Grace, who went to meet him in his hotel with Adit, Ajay refused to budge. He sat alone in his hotel room and drank the whole day.

Chapter 5

In the days following the hotel visit, Adit's personality changed dramatically. He became reticent and thoughtful. He sat for hours in the library, holding the yellow toy bus, looking out the window at the contractor digging the land. There was a permanent worried look on Adit's face.

On the day of Adit's appointment with Dr Ratnakar, Seema landed at the Rastogi Mansion and surprised Grace and Vijay.

"How come you are here?" asked Vijay

Before Seema could respond, Om appeared and escorted her inside. "Raju, see who has come!" he shouted as he made her sit at the dining table. When Raju Kaka saw her, he was thrilled. He hugged her and asked, "Now that you have returned, I hope you are not going back."

"It all depends on Vijay, Kaka," laughed Seema. Then she turned towards Vijay and said, "When you meet your lover after many years, the question should not be, 'How come you are here?' It should be 'How are you?'"

A visibly embarrassed but internally happy Vijay apologised to Seema. After Kaka had served her favourite breakfast and everyone had left Vijay and Seema to catch up, Vijay asked her, "How have you been?"

Seema smiled and said, "I was married against my will but left the husband on my own free will. My dad never accepted me back when I returned, so I stayed in a ladies hostel near the hospital where I work. The divorce took a toll on dad, and he passed away three months after my return. He had not written a will, but I inherited everything since I was the only child. I sent you many messages, but you refused to respond, so I stopped communicating. Your father kept in touch and updated me on everything, including Ajay's arrival, his closeness with Abhinav, and his leaving home. I met him the other day in town; he was high at 11:00 a.m. We sat in a coffee shop where we had coffee; I had a cappuccino while he laced his with whiskey. He told me that Grace and you are having an affair and that Abhinav was siphoning money out from his account. He also told me that he was cursed and his work was not progressing. What is wrong with him?"

"He is in the wrong company. I told him to stay away from Abhinav, but he did not listen. Now, the alcohol is killing him. Anyway, you look radiant as ever," Vijay said.

"Am I? Good. Your dad told me to maintain my health and figure as he plans to get us married." Seema's direct response surprised Vijay.

"Oh, I wasn't aware that you two had planned so far ahead," Vijay said with a smile.

Seema realised that Vijay was at a loss for words, so she changed the topic. She held his hand and asked, "What is wrong with Adit?"

"I don't know. After getting slapped by Ajay, he changed a bit, but lately, he is stuck with that yellow toy bus, and he keeps staring at the workers angrily. Somehow, I feel he is upset with this whole digging bit."

"He may be upset that his play area is gone. Don't think too much about it. Sometimes, children take certain things very seriously. But nothing a little bit of therapy can't cure," said Seema, patting his hand reassuringly.

The two of them were still chatting when they heard Om's shout and a crash. Vijay and Seema ran towards the sound and saw Om on the floor in the corridor. The ceramic flower vase in the corridor was broken, and pieces were scattered everywhere.

"What happened?" Vijay asked as they helped Om stand up.

"I think the stupid Raju dropped cooking oil on the floor. I heard Adit calling me and was rushing towards the living room when I slipped on the oil and fell."

"How are you feeling?" asked Seema

"I think I have sprained my ankle," said Om as he was finding it difficult to put his right leg down.

Vijay picked up Om and took him to his bedroom, Seema followed him. After putting him on the bed, Vijay told Seema, "Looks like I will need to be here. I will cancel Adit's appointment.

Seema intervened and said, "No need to cancel. I will take him. You take care of Babuji."

Just then, Adit walked in. He was holding his yellow toy bus in his right hand. "What happened to Dadu?" he asked sweetly.

As Vijay turned to answer Adit, he saw Seema looking at the child strangely. Her look was a mix of respect and fear. Her eyelids blinked a few times rapidly as he watched her, and then she sat down on a chair, looking a little tired.

"Are you okay?" asked Vijay.

Seema took a moment to gather herself and said, "Just a sudden blood rush. I am perfectly fine." She looked at Adit, who was looking intently at her. Suddenly, he smiled. Seema smiled back and asked, "Will you come with Seema Aunty to see the doctor?"

"Will you buy me an ice cream after meeting the doctor?" Adit asked, looking at Seema.

"Of course," Seema laughed as she picked him up and started walking out of the house. As they were leaving, they crossed Grace, who was coming out of the room. She saw Seema carrying Adit. She smiled and tried to remove the yellow toy bus from Adit's hand, saying, "Don't take that to the doctor, son," but Seema grabbed Grace's wrist in a flash and moved it away from Adit. "Let it be. It is a part of him," she said sternly.

Taken aback by Seema's aggressive reaction, Grace stepped back without saying anything.

After they left, she showed Vijay the red welts on her wrist and asked, "What was that?"

"I don't know. Never seen her behave like that," said Vijay, inspecting the welts.

"Be careful; she has a stronghold," laughed Grace.

***

At the hospital, Dr Ratnakar inspected Adit thoroughly. He also took him for a one-on-one psychological evaluation and then returned after an hour and said, "His behaviour is perfectly normal, but somehow, I feel there is something wrong. I will need to do a few more tests on him. I will inform Vijay, but can you get Adit tomorrow, please?"

"Sure," said Seema casually. She had decided not to bring Adit back because she felt nothing was wrong with him. As they left, a woman holding a kid entered the room. Seema noticed that she looked agitated, and the boy's eyes kept rolling back often to show the white of his eyes. "What is wrong with him?" she asked the mother.

"He is suffering from Nystagmus—a vision condition in which the eyes make repetitive, uncontrolled movements. These movements often reduce vision and depth perception, affecting balance and coordination. These involuntary eye movements can occur from side to side, up and down, or in a circular pattern," said Dr Ratnakar, who had overheard Seema asking the lady about her son. Then he looked at the lady and said, "I recommend you meet our neuro-ophthalmologist, Dr Ruby, on the first floor."

The lady glared at Dr Ratnakar. "I am coming from her. She asked me to meet you. Can one of you decide what is wrong with my son, or will the two of you keep playing ping pong with us?" she shouted.

Realising there would be some debate between Ratnakar and the lady, Seema excused herself and left with Adit.

As they passed the cafeteria, Adit asked, "Ice cream?"

Seema nodded and walked into the cafeteria. When they entered, she made Adit sit at a table and went to the cafe counter to buy him an ice cream. After returning with the ice cream, she opened her bag to take out her car keys but found them to be missing.

"Now, where did I leave the car keys?" she asked loudly.

"I think you left it on the doctor's table," said Adit as he licked his ice cream.

"You wait here. I will be back in a minute with the keys," she said. As she walked to the doctor's office, her eyelids started blinking rapidly again. Adit watched her enter Dr Ratnakar's cabin, looked at his ice cream and smiled. After about ten minutes, she stepped out of the cabin, walked back to Adit, picked him up and left. Once they got into the car, she called Vijay and said, "We are finished here and are leaving now. See you soon."

Chapter 6

When Seema and Adit reached home an hour later, she met Vijay and Grace, who were having tea in the dining room.

"How did it go?" Vijay asked

"He is perfectly fine. He needs some rest for a few days, lots of love and affection, and he will return to normal." Then she looked at Grace and said, "You will have to take a week's leave and be with him."

"Oh no! The British Foreign Minister is coming this week; hence, all leaves are cancelled," said Grace.

"What do we do?" Asked Vijay.

Grace looked mischievously at Vijay, then turned to Seema with a knowing smile and asked, "Can you stay for a week with us, please?"

"Can you do that?" asked Vijay with a pleading look.

"I have my patients and a home to care of, " Seema replied with a smile.

"Please understand our situation, Seema," pleaded Grace as she held Seema's hands.

Seema looked at the welts on Grace's wrist and asked softly, "Did I do that?"

Grace looked at the welts and smiled, "It's okay."

Seema's eyes moistened as she traced her fingers over the welts and said softly, "I have hurt you, and to make up for that, I agree to stay here till Adit gets better."

"Yippee," said Grace as they all hugged each other. That night, Vijay helped Seema move into a room on the second floor next to Grace and Adit's bedroom in the Rastogi Mansion.

The next day in the late evening, Inspector Majid Khan from the local Police Station dropped in at the Rastogi Mansion. When Majid walked in, Vijay, Grace, and Seema were chatting in the living room while Adit was playing with his yellow bus in his room.

"How can we help you, Mr Khan?" Vijay asked, a little irritated that Majid had walked into the house unannounced.

"Dr Ratnakar is dead," he said, looking at Seema.

Vijay and Grace looked shocked. "When?" asked Vijay

"Yesterday, after he met with Ms Seema Kashyap and her son Adit," said Majid, walking up to Seema.

"How did he die?" asked Grace.

"Someone stabbed him in his kidney and then ripped his throat," he said, his eyes still directed at Seema.

"But why are you here? You are not saying that Dr Kashyap killed her colleague in his cabin?" asked Vijay, coming in between Seema and Majid.

"The CCTV footage shows Dr Kashyap was the last one to meet him," Majid said, handing Vijay a screenshot of the CCTV.

Seema looked at the picture briefly and said, "A lady with her son met with Dr Ratnakar after we left."

"Yes, but they left before you returned to his cabin," Majid said, showing two more pictures of the mother and child leaving and Seema entering again.

"I forgot my car keys in his room, so I returned, picked it up and left. I did not kill anyone. Just because I was the last to be seen on a CCTV footage, I become the killer? I have no motive. Why should I kill him?" asked Seema.

"That is what I am here to discover, Dr Kashyap." Replied Majid calmly.

Before Majid could ask anything more, Grace said, "Aren't there any clues? Like footprints, hand prints, etc?"

"None. The killer was a professional. *She* used gloves and fabric foot covers used in hospitals. Someone who knew about these things."

"What about a murder weapon?" asked Vijay

"Like I said, the killer was clever. She used an icicle as a murder weapon."

"How did you arrive at that conclusion?"

"I have been solving murders for twenty years. There was a large pool of ice-cold water. Dr Ratnakar's freezer had a problem with defrosting, and there were icicles in the freezer."

He showed another picture of the freezer and said, "Someone broke a big icicle and used that as a weapon." Majid explained, "The killer stabbed him in the kidney when he was in his inner cabin with a frozen stick of ice that was taken from the fridge, and when he went down in pain, slit the doctor's jugular vein. The killer then dropped the murder weapon on the floor, which melted within seconds when it got mixed with the warm blood of the good doctor. The cut to the throat is precise like how a surgeon does with a scalpel," said Majid, staring at Seema.

"Listen, Inspector Khan, Dr Kashyap is a reputed Paediatric Surgeon who is well known in the society. Vijay requested that she take Adit to the hospital as I was unwell, so she had no motive. Everything you said is pure conjecture, so if you don't have any evidence, please leave," said Om, who had walked into the room.

"Of course, Mr Rastogi, I have no intentions of staying back. But I will come back, and that too, with evidence," said Majid.

"Stay away from Seema Aunty," blurted Adit from the corner. Everyone was shocked at his boldness.

After Majid left, Vijay hugged Adit and said, "You are brave, Chote Nawab," Grace kissed him and said to Seema, "You have started having a positive effect on my son. Thank you."

With Grace and Vijay busy with heavy workloads, Seema being at home was a boon for everyone as she managed Adit, Om, and even the house. On Om's request, she took a three-month sabbatical from work. Seema took charge of the house as time passed, and Adit spent considerable time with her. They ate, played, and slept together. Adit, his yellow bus, and Seema were so inseparable that one day during breakfast, Grace jokingly said, "I don't know if I am Adit's mother or you. He is always with you, and you also behave like a kid."

"You are right. If you notice, Seema plays with the yellow bus even after putting Adit to bed," laughed Vijay.

"But Seema has always been a kid since I have known her. She loved toys. In fact, she would hide her toys in the attic and ask for more from her father," said Om with a warm smile.

"All that is fine, but haven't you two forgotten something?" asked Grace.

"What?" Vijay and Seema asked in unison.

"You had planned to go to a movie today; morning show, remember? And you have just half an hour left," said Grace.

"Oh shit. I completely forgot," said Vijay as he dragged Seema out of her chair. "Don't forget to make my paneer tikka masala Kaka," shouted Seema as she and Vijay ran out of the house. Seeing them panic, all of them started laughing.

Chapter 7

A few days later, one evening, when Vijay, Grace and Om went grocery shopping, Raju Kaka was cooking dinner. He heard a male voice from the library. Wondering who it could be, he walked down to the basement. As he got closer to the library, the voices became clearer. A man was ordering something, and a woman in a soft voice was responding.

When Raju Kaka opened the door and entered the library, it was dark, except for a light falling from a low-wattage bulb above the red velvet chair. On the chair, he saw Adit sitting with his legs over the armrest and looking at something opposite.

"What are you doing here alone, Chote Nawab?" asked Raju Kaka.

In response, a male voice answered from behind the bookshelves, "You shouldn't have come, Kaka."

As his eyes searched for the voice's owner, a man's shadow suddenly started falling over Adit. Frightened, he turned to run out of the room, but suddenly, a heavy wooden bookshelf next to the entrance door came crashing on him, breaking his spine just below the neck, killing him instantly.

A frightened Adit ran out of the room shouting, "Chachu, Chachu," since everyone was out, Seema came running from her room and asked, "What happened?"

Adit pointed to the library. He was at a loss for words. As Seema cautiously approached the steps down to the library, she heard some sound coming from the living room. She ran towards the noise only to find that Vijay, Grace and Om had returned from shopping. When she told them about Adit's scream and his pointing towards the library, they all went to see what happened.

Vijay led the way as they went down the steps. He slowly opened the library door, peeped in and saw Raju Kaka's body lying under the bookshelf and said, "Oh my god."

Kaka's death was a big blow to the family as he had been with the Rastogis since the time of Ram Prakash. He had come to them as a child. When the news reached Ajay, he even sacrificed his alcohol for a day and participated in the last rites of Kaka. After the funeral, Grace met with Ajay and said, "If you can give up the alcohol for a day, you can give it up completely. That Abhinav has poisoned your mind and created a rift between us. Come back home."

A sober Ajay broke down. "Abhinav has fleeced me of all the money, and my dream to do business has gone to the dogs. Because of him, I lost everything, including you and Adit."

"It's never too late. Confront Abhinav and ask him for your money. Then split with him and come back home," said Grace.

"Yes, yes. I will do that at the right time. I will confront him," said Ajay. Though he did not sound convincing, Grace let him go.

That night, after Ajay left, Seema cooked dinner for everyone. After a quiet dinner, Om and Vijay sat in the living room; Kaka's death had a profound effect on Om who started thinking of his own death. Om said to Vijay, "I don't know how much time I have left. I think the time has come for you to get married to Seema. Let me at least see my grandson before I die, Vijay."

"I agree, Babuji. Please talk to her and fix a date," replied Vijay, knowing very well that Seema would never say no.

Thrilled with Vijay and Seema's consent, Om organised a Roka ceremony for Vijay and Seema a month later, which friends and close relatives attended. Songs, dances and a sumptuous lunch added joy to the festivities. After a long time, the house was alive with music and laughter, and everyone found an opportunity to let their hair down. The party dragged on until night, and by the time everyone left, it was already 11:00 p.m. After everyone left, Vijay retired to his library to write a new poem on their engagement. He was so engrossed in his poetry that he did not notice Adit, who had entered and was standing next to him. "What are you doing, Chachu?" he asked, jolting Vijay out of his wits.

Though shaken by Adit's sudden presence, Vijay looked at his cute face, smiled, and asked, "Why are you not in bed, Chote Nawab?"

"Not feeling sleepy, Chachu; what are you writing?" he asked, peeping into the pages.

"I am writing an Urdu poem on our Roka."

"I also love Urdu poetry," said Adit.

Vijay looked at him mischievously and asked, "Seriously? You can read Urdu?"

"Yes, Chachu, I know Urdu poetry," Adit insisted.

Vijay put down his pen and said, "Accha, then narrate one to me."

Adit walked across, sat on the red velvet chair, and recited an Urdu poem. Mesmerised by the lyrics and the recitation, Vijay looked at Adit in wonder and asked softly, "Who taught you this?"

Adit smiled, pecked Chachu on the cheek, and said, "My secret. Good night, Chachu." As he walked away, Vijay looked at Adit in disbelief. A few minutes later, Seema walked into the library, sat on Vijay's lap, and said, "Now that we are engaged, can we sleep together?"

"Technically, no." He smiled, carried Seema to his bed, and said, "Emotionally, yes."

After making love to each other that night, they lay in bed and looked at the full moon outside in the sky. Vijay told Seema about Adit's Urdu Poetry recitation.

"Of course, he is talented. His grandfather was an Urdu poet, did you not know?" asked Seema sarcastically, referring to Om Prakash.

"No, I did not know", said Vijay, crushing her in his arms.

While Vijay and Seema's romance bloomed, Ajay's frustration increased by the day due to excessive delays in the foundation construction. After a week of waiting, one day, Ajay lost his cool.

"I am fed up with your excuses and tardiness. I will give you one week. If the foundation is not ready by then, I will sack you. I am holding back the payments until I see the job completed," Ajay screamed at the contractor.

The scared contractor folded his hands and said, "I promise I will finish this within this week and begin the column and roof work simultaneously. We will complete the project in one month, saab."

"One month. Not a single day more," said Ajay and walked off.

The contractor sighed in relief and left to arrange for more workers. Just as he crossed one-half of the main road, a red Hyundai i20 came racing towards him. To avoid getting hit by the vehicle, the contractor jumped backwards and in front of a speeding truck from the other side. The truck hit him so hard that he was flung six feet in the air before he crashed on the sidewalk with a broken skull. While the red i20 sped away, oblivious to what had happened, the frightened truck driver sped off, hoping to escape the scene. Unfortunately for both, everything was captured on the CCTV camera positioned on the lamp posts.

Chapter 8

That evening, when Inspector Majid Khan arrived at the Rastogi Mansion again, Om was sleeping, and Vijay and Grace had still not returned from the office as they were working overtime. Seema was in her room on the second floor, with her headphones on, doing aerobics while Adit played with the yellow bus in a corner, so she never realised Majid's presence until he entered the room.

Seeing Majid inside her bedroom, a shocked and angry Seema shouted at Majid, "How dare you enter my bedroom? How dare you enter the house without knocking? This is not your Police station that you can walk in any time unannounced. Get out. Get out now," she screamed. A terrified Adit stopped playing and quietly sat on the bed.

"I rang the bell many times, but no one answered. I heard music from here, so I came up. My apologies," he said, stepping out of the room and back onto the second-floor veranda.

"What are you here for now?" Shouted Seema.

"Mr Ajay's contractor was killed today. He was hit by a truck." Majid said, leaning his back on the veranda railings.

"Ajay stays in a hotel. Go ask him," she snapped.

"But the CCTV footage shows you trying to run him over with your i20. When he avoided you and jumped back, he got hit by the truck," said Majid, extending his phone towards her in an attempt to show her the video of a speeding red car.

She peered at the video and said, "Yes, that is my car, and I was in a hurry to reach the hospital. I had Adit with me, too. Do you think I will try to run over a man with a child in the car? Are you crazy, or do you have an axe to grind with me?" she snapped.

"Please, Dr Kashyap, wait..." Majid reached out and held Seema's hand even as she turned to return to her room.

"How dare you hold my hand!" Seema shouted. She yanked her hand out of his grasp and slapped him hard on his left cheek. The slap was so powerful that Majid stumbled backward. He tried to hold the railings for support, missed, lost his balance and went over it. As his body hurtled down from the second floor, Majid screamed for a few seconds before he fell headlong onto the central stone courtyard. His head hit the stones first and then his body. By the time Seema ran down the stairs to check on him, he was dead. She looked at Majid's dead body, then at Adit, who was looking down at her from the second-floor veranda. When she saw Om, who had come running, hearing the noise, she started crying. "It was an accident, Babuji; I never meant to kill him," she wailed, holding her head in her arms.

"What happened?" asked Om as he rushed to Seema's side.

"I was exercising when he suddenly entered my room and started questioning me about the death of Ajay's contractor. I told him I didn't know anything about his death, but he tried to drag me. I pulled out of his grasp and slapped him. He lost his balance and went over the railing. Oh my god, what will I do now?" she sobbed.

"It is not your fault," said Om. After thinking for a while, he called Majid's boss, CI Rajshekhar, and said, "There has been a fatal accident in my house. Please come quickly." Then he called

Vijay and Grace and told them what had happened. By the time Rajshekhar arrived, Vijay and Grace had also reached home.

When CI Rajshekhar arrived, he asked Om who all the witnesses were to the crime.

"She and the child," he answered, pointing upwards.

CI Rajshekhar looked up at Adit on the second-floor balcony and smiled. Then he climbed up to Adit and asked him, "What happened, Beta?"

Adit looked down at Majid's dead body, then at Seema, and said softly, "Seema Aunty was exercising, and that uncle came inside the room. He shouted at Seema Aunty and tried to drag her, but he slipped and fell backwards."

"Thank you, beta," said CI Raj. He came down and asked Seema if that was what had happened.

Seema looked at Om, who nodded at her. She looked at Adit and then said to CI Rajshekhar, "Yes,"

"Why did he come here?" asked CI Rajshekhar.

Seema explained the reason and told him about the video. "After showing me the video, he yanked my hand but slipped and went over."

CI Rajshekhar looked at the video and said, "You are at fault for driving rashly, but I cannot say you killed the contractor. Also, this death looks like an accident, too. Anyway, thanks for the cooperation. I will get back to you. Please do not leave the city till the investigations are over."

Chapter 9

Several weeks passed, and it became clear that there were no direct charges against Seema, so CI Rajshekhar made her pay a fine for negligent driving and closed the case as an accidental death. The truck driver who had run over the contractor was caught, charged with involuntary manslaughter, and sentenced to five years in prison.

With all issues cleared out, Om fixed the date for Seema and Vijay's wedding. Just as the entire house got busy with shopping and other preparations for the wedding, a bank notice arrived in Ajay's name stating his company had defaulted on loan payment. Om called Ajay and questioned him but soon realised his son was ignorant of the loan. Realising that Abhinav had used the power of attorney given to him by Ajay and taken a big loan without informing Ajay, an angry Om decided to take things into his own hands and called Abhinav. "I want the entire expense sheet of Ajay's company by tomorrow at my residence, or I will file a criminal case against you," said Om.

An angry Abhinav retorted, "Fine, I will bring it over tomorrow."

The next day, Abhinav arrived unannounced in the evening. Om and Vijay had gone grocery shopping, Seema and Adit were at her hospital, and Grace was alone at home.

Having rung the bell with no response, Abhinav was about to leave when he saw that the front door was unlocked. As he opened and entered the house, he saw the silhouette of Grace in the window upstairs. She had stepped out of a bath and was naked. Lured by uncontrollable lust, he quickly ran up the stairs and opened her bedroom door.

Before she could react, he locked it from the inside and grabbed her naked body. Grace screamed for help and tried to fight back, but Abhinav was powerful. He twisted her arms behind her and tied them with a towel. As he pushed her on the bed and prepared to ravage her, the bedroom door burst open. Abhinav whirled around and saw Seema and Adit standing in the doorway. Seema had a pair of giant scissors in her hand. Abhinav sidestepped as she pounced on him and ran out of the room. Seema chased him, screaming, but he managed to escape somehow. When she returned and untied her, a grateful Grace hugged Seema and thanked her profusely for saving her life and reputation.

When Om and Vijay returned and heard about Abhinav's attack on Grace, Vijay got livid and decided to teach him a lesson, but Seema stopped him and advised him to file an FIR. When Vijay reached the Police station, he was told that CI Rajshekhar had been transferred and SI Manik Chand, Majid's replacement, was in charge. Vijay asked the SI to lodge an FIR, but to his shock, the SI refused and threatened him that he would reopen Seema's case again. A worried Vijay made discreet enquiries and discovered that Manik was Abhinav's friend and on his payroll. Frustrated by the outcome, Vijay was returning home when he bumped into a haggard and tired-looking Ajay. Seeing his irresponsible brother, Vijay lost his temper and said to him, "Your partner screwed you, and you kept quiet; last night, he tried to rape your wife, and you are still busy getting drunk. Shame on you."

Shattered by Vijay's accusations, Ajay called Abhinav and said, "Let's meet at the site tonight. It's been a while since we got together. We will have a few drinks and then go for dinner."

Though surprised by the invitation, Abhinav agreed.

After speaking to Abhinav, Ajay called Grace. When she answered, he said, "I have been a bad husband and a disgraceful father, but if you can forgive me, I will make everything alright."

"Oh, Ajay. I am so happy you called. Adit and I will always be there for you. Just stop drinking and get out of this loan mess," she replied.

***

That night, when Abhinav met Ajay at the site, it was almost 10:00 p.m., and everyone in the Rastogi Mansion was fast asleep. They met at the far end of the site. Ajay, already a few drinks down, lit a nice bonfire and ordered some snacks. Initially, both were cordial and discussed various things pertaining to business, but as the conversation progressed towards the finances, the discussions started to heat up. At one point, Ajay lost his cool and stood up, "You screwed me financially, you created a rift between me and my brother by your lies and now you have eyes on Grace? I will kill you, you bastard," shouted Ajay.

In the mansion, Vijay and Grace heard Ajay shouting and abusing Abhinav. Vijay pulled on his sweater and was about to go and see what was happening at the site when Grace said, "I am coming with you. He will listen to me."

In the meantime, at the site, Abhinav, also drunk, stood up and said, "If that Seema hadn't come, I would have raped your English wife twice over."

A livid Ajay leaned forward and slapped Abhinav hard on his left cheek. Stunned by the sudden assault, Abhinav took time to react; but when he stepped forward to counterattack, he stumbled and fell headlong into the bonfire. As the flames licked his body, Abhinav screamed in agony. By the time Vijay and Grace reached the site, half of Abhinav's body was on fire.

"What did you do, Ajay?" asked Grace, seeing Abhinav's burning body.

"I did not do anything, Grace. I just slapped him, and he stumbled over into the fire. I had no intentions of killing him. Please believe me," he pleaded.

Vijay tried his level best to drag Abhinav's body from the fire, but Abhinav was a heavy man. Luckily, Seema arrived and helped him. Together, they held Abhinav by his feet, dragged him out of the bonfire and doused the fire on his body by throwing sand and mud.

Vijay immediately called an ambulance and informed SI Manik Chand. Both arrived within minutes. As the medics picked up Abhinav to put him on a stretcher, one of them turned to look at SI Manik Chand and shook his head—Abhinav had succumbed to his burns and died. As they were loading Abhinav's body into the van, SI Manik Chand tapped Vijay and pointed at Abhinav's feet.

The shoelaces on both legs were tied together.

"This is not an accident, as you made me believe. Someone tied his laces together so that he would stumble into the fire. This is murder, and right now, my suspect is Ajay Rastogi," said SI Manik Chand as he grabbed Ajay and pushed him into the Police Jeep.

After hearing all the commotion, Om and Adit had also come running to the site. Seeing Ajay being taken away by the cops, Om held his head in his hands and sobbed, "See where his rebellion has led him to. My son is a murderer."

***

After 14 days in Police custody, Ajay was found guilty of murder in the first degree and sentenced to life imprisonment. The entire Rastogi family was so devastated by the verdict that a sense of gloom prevailed over the house for weeks till Seema took control of the situation.

"Listen, what had to happen has happened. Though we all feel bad for Ajay and miss him, our moroseness and depression are affecting Adit. At least for him, we should get back to normal life."

Everyone realised Seema was right and slowly returned to their old routine. After Abhinav's death, the power of attorney held no value, so, the property was returned to Ajay, who wrote it back to Om. Vijay filled the excavated area and planted grass. In a few months, the lawns started looking green, and Rastogi Mansion slowly began to return to life. Grace and Vijay had started going back to work. Surprisingly, Adit recovered the fastest and returned to his happy self, but he was still stuck to Seema and his yellow bus.

One day, after dinner, Om said to Vijay, "The past year has been traumatic. So many deaths have occurred since Ajay's return to India. It all started with Dr Ratnakar's murder when Adit was taken to the hospital. Then Kaka died, followed by Ajay's contractor, who died in the freak accident. SI Majid's death followed it, and then came Ajay's partner—Abhinav's gruesome death. Somehow, I feel they are all linked. Someone wanted to punish Ajay, and they finally managed it."

"Babuji, who in this family will want to punish Ajay? And for what? Who stands to win by his imprisonment?" asked Vijay.

Just then, Grace walked up and wished them good night. As she left, Om and Vijay looked at each other. Since the seed of suspicion had been sown, Vijay felt it was only right to investigate what Om had said, so he went and met Ajay in the prison. After telling him what Om had said, he asked Ajay for his opinion.

"While I agree with Babuji that someone really wanted to get me here, I don't think it is Grace. She still loves me and meets me every week without telling you all. In fact, she also told me something similar, but her theory was slightly different. She feels things took a downturn after Seema arrived at the house."

A visibly upset Vijay was about to argue when Ajay intervened and said, "I also got upset with Grace initially but realised she was not blaming Seema. Instead, Grace felt that someone was after her. Someone who does not want her to get married to you. Someone who wants you to believe she is a bad omen for the Rastogis."

"Why does she feel that way?" asked Vijay.

"Look at all the deaths. None of it was her doing, but it all happened when she was around. You met her after a long time, sparks flew, but everything took a back seat with Dr Ratnakar's murder; you asked her to take Adit to him, and when he was killed, the suspicion fell on her. By the time she got out of that mess and you two started dating, the contractor died. I screamed at the contractor that day; he got worked up and absentmindedly walked into the middle of the road; a truck killed him, but Seema came under suspicion again. When she recovered and you two got engaged, SI Majid died. Luckily, Adit saw it happen, so we know Seema was innocent. And now Abinav got burnt to death. This time, she wasn't even there, but thanks to the tragedy and me on death row, your wedding has been cancelled again. Trust me, Grace is right. Someone is after Seema."

A confused Vijay returned home and spoke to Om. "Ajay also has a point. If that is the case, then my son is innocent. Let's investigate this thoroughly and see who is Abhinav's real murderer. I will explore things my way. In the meantime, you better converse with Seema when you feel the time is right.

***

A few days later, Vijay went to Seema's room to chat with her. When he entered, she was having a bath, so he decided to potter around the room. Looking around, he saw Adit's yellow bus on her table. As he picked it up, Seema came out of the bathroom. She gave him a look of pleasant surprise and asked, "How come my future husband is here?"

"As your future husband, I have every right to be here," he joked while he waved the yellow bus at her and asked, "What is this doing here? I thought Adit could never stay without it."

"Oh the bus; well, he left it here a week ago. He is a big boy now, Vijay; he no longer comes to my room or spends time with me. He is busy reading poetry. He keeps taking books from your library and spends hours with them. Looks like he has his ancestor's genes in him. He was the only friend I had when you all were busy; now even he has moved on," she said as she changed into a pair of pants and a shirt.

"Come on, Seema. He is eight years old. In another ten years, he will finish high school and leave all of us." Seeing a sad look in Seema's eyes, Vijay forgot that he had come up to talk to her about the deaths and whether she had any enemies. He hugged her affectionately and said, "Let us forget everything and go out shopping."

"What is the occasion?"

"Our wedding."

"But I thought it got cancelled for now," she said.

"Well, I revived it again."

"When?"

"Just now."

"What about Babuji?"

"I will manage him. Come, let's go shopping. You can decide on your wedding dress while I buy some books from Jain Bookstores." Vijay dragged her out of the house and left.

Chapter 10

After dropping Seema off at a famous shop specialising in wedding clothes, Vijay reached Jain Bookstores and met his friend Pradeep Jain, the owner's son, who was now in charge of the bookshop. Over a cup of coffee, he told Pradeep, "My wedding is coming up, and I want to hold a Mushaira on the night of the reception. I have written a few poems, but I also want to recite some Urdu poems that no one has ever read. It is not necessary that it has to be a famous poet. It just has to be a set of unheard poems. Can you help me?"

Pradeep thought for a while and said, "Look, neither my dad nor I are into Urdu poems, but I remember my grandfather giving him some Urdu poetry books."

"Is it by some famous poet?" asked Vijay.

"No. These are poems by a local poet called Mirza. He wrote them as a hobby. Post-partition, he moved to Pakistan and left behind all his books. The government handed them over to my grandfather as he was the only local bookshop owner. As I said, the poet is not famous, but I can guarantee the poems are unheard of as they were never published. It is just a handwritten brown diary."

"Where are they?" asked Vijay.

"They are lying in the back somewhere. If you find it, take it home. I have no need for them."

Vijay searched the dusty shelves for an hour and finally found the diary. It was a brown leather diary that was half-burnt. 'It could have got burnt in the fire,' he thought. After thanking Pradeep, he left with the brown diary, picked up Seema, and went home.

***

While Vijay and Seema were shopping, Om prakash was conducting his own investigation. He recorded everything that had happened chronologically from when he received Grace's first message, saying Adit was born. Then he tried to see if there was anything linking all the deaths and various incidents but found none. There were some unanswered questions in his mind, though. *'Who killed Dr Ratnakar and why? Was Raju Kaka's death, the contractor's death and Majid Khan's death mere accidents or deliberate murders? Who tied Abhinav's laces?'*

The only link he could establish through all this was that Seema was present in all incidents except Raju Kaka and Abhinav's death. Not knowing what to do, he decided to begin with Seema. He started observing her. The more he observed her, the more he found her habits intriguing. Though an unmarried guest in his house, she behaved like a daughter-in-law. She had completely controlled the house and was very close to Adit. He noticed that they spent hours talking to each other in her room. And as days passed, he noticed she played with the yellow bus more than Adit. In fact, he saw her holding the bus and talking to it as she sat on the lawn by herself. One day, after dinner, he asked Vijay to meet him on the lawns. Once they were alone, he told Vijay about all his observations. "There is something wrong, but I cannot put my finger on the pulse," said Om.

***

That night after dinner, Seema, dressed in a silk full-length nightie, said to Vijay, "Tonight we will make love as we have never done before,"

"Not tonight. I have to review some books I bought from the bookshop. You go to sleep," said Vijay. Seema looked at him with disappointment and went back to her room.

After she left, Vijay went to the library, opened the brown diary from the bookshop, and started reading the poems. His excitement grew as he flipped each page, and noticed that the poems were excellent. He had reached only the sixth page when a black-and-white photograph slipped from the book and fell to the floor. He picked it up and looked at the picture. It had become yellow and grainy with age, but he could see a young man sitting with a one-year-old boy on his lap. The boy was holding a toy bus. To the man's left stood a young woman, probably his wife. To the right of the man, the picture was torn. As though someone was in the photo but had been removed. From the size of the tear, and a part of a women's dress that was visible, it looked like the missing person was also a grown woman. Curious, Vijay carefully took a magnifying glass from his shelf and studied the picture. Two things shocked him. One, the room where the picture was taken was the same library he was sitting in, and two, the number plate on the toy bus was the same as the one on the yellow bus Adit played with.

Vijay's hands started shaking, and beads of sweat started appearing on his forehead. He licked his dry lips, looked out the window for a few seconds, and rushed to Om. When Vijay entered Om's room, he found him watching the late-night news on TV. He shut the door behind him, sat beside Om, showed him the picture, and asked, "Do you recognise anything?"

Om looked at the picture and shook his head. Vijay gave him the magnifying glass and said, "Now look."

Om carefully studied the picture under the lens and said casually, "This is the picture of the young Mirza family."

"Are you sure?" Vijay asked.

"Of course, I am sure. This picture was on the library wall when my father bought the house. At that time, it was not a library. It was a basement where the family did Namaz. Where did you get it from?" asked Om.

"Forget that. Look at the bus the woman is holding. It is the same as the one Adit found during the excavation and he has been carrying around."

"Must be a coincidence," said Om.

"No, the number plate on the bus is the same as the one we have, unless that also is a strange coincidence," Vijay said, putting the picture down.

"Does the woman resemble anyone here?" asked Om.

"No, she does not resemble Seema," snapped Vijay as he knew what Om was trying to hint.

"Hmm… then the common link I have been looking for is the yellow Bus," said Om.

"What do you mean?" asked Vijay

"It was after the bus was discovered that Adit started behaving strangely; even Seema's behaviour seemed strange when Grace tried to take the bus away. When Adit was addicted to the bus, his behaviour changed; now Seema is stuck with the bus," said Om.

"But she's not behaving strangely. I think you are obsessed with her. Initially, you tried to convince me that Seema is behind everything, but now it is a plastic toy creating problems for us. You keep shifting your goal post because you don't believe your son Ajay is the root cause of all these issues." Vijay got up and left the room, leaving the picture on Om's bed.

After Vijay left, Om looked at the picture and said softly, "I will destroy the yellow bus without anyone's knowledge. Let us see if things improve after that."

Chapter 11

The next day, when everyone left for work, Om decided to try to confiscate the toy bus. He first went to Adit's room and searched for the bus but could not find it. Then he went up to Seema's room, but the room was locked. He peeped through the window panes on the door and saw the bus kept on a shelf. A disgruntled Om decided to make another attempt in the evening when she returned from work.

Om did not disclose his plans to Vijay or Grace when they returned home after work. He waited for Seema to come home and Vijay and Grace to retire to their rooms. Once he was sure that Seema had gone for a bath, he went upstairs to her room. He opened the door and tiptoed in. He could hear Seema humming a song in the bathroom. Relieved, he picked up the yellow toy bus and was about to leave her room when Seema said from behind, "Where are you taking that bus, Babuji?"

Om whirled around and saw Seema standing beside her writing table with a big smile. Her hair was still wet, and she was wearing an off-white silk nightie. "Where are you taking my bus?" she asked. Om noticed that her tone had changed and sounded angry.

"I... I am taking it to play with Adit," stuttered Om.

"He does not need it anymore. Give it back to me," she said sternly.

Om moved his hand, holding the bus behind his back, and said, "It…it belongs to Adit, and I am giving it to him." Then he stepped back.

Suddenly, Seema's face contorted, and in a dual-tone voice, said, "Give me the toy." Om noticed she had a pair of scissors in her hand and was inflicting a wound on herself as she kept slashing her right thigh while talking to him. Om watched the blood from the thigh wound spread onto the nightie and drip down on the floor. Though scared, he put up a brave front and asked her, "Who are you?"

"Your death," she screamed in a dual-tone voice as she charged at him with the scissors. The sound of the scream jolted everyone. Vijay, Grace and Adit all came running out of their rooms. As Vijay and Grace stood in the central courtyard and looked up, they saw Om running along the second-floor corridor with the yellow toy bus in his hand with Seema, bleeding from her right leg, screaming and chasing him with a pair of scissors in her hand. As Vijay took the stairs on the left, Grace ran up the stairs on the right. Om realised he would never reach any of the stairs, so he dived into one of the empty rooms and bolted it from the inside, even as a screaming Seema started kicking the door with her bleeding right leg. "I will kill you tonight, I will kill you tonight…" she kept repeating as she yanked and kicked at the door.

A frightened Adit watched all this, standing opposite from his room on the first floor. Suddenly, Seema went silent. She turned around, her contorted face looking first at Grace—approaching her from the left and Vijay from the right. Realising she was boxed in, she gave one last growl and looked down the balcony.

"No, Seema…no," pleaded Vijay, tears streaming down his cheeks, but before Grace or Vijay could reach her, she jumped over the balcony railing with a shrill scream. Her body hit the concrete floor with a loud thud.

When Vijay and Grace reached her side, she was breathing, returned to her normal self, but her fading look told Vijay she was about to die.

"Why Seema, why did you do all this?" asked Vijay, cradling her head in his arms.

"It is all written in my red diary. Forgive me, Vijay. I have always loved you." And then her body went still.

Vijay held Seema tightly and wailed loudly. Grace and Om tried to console him, but he was inconsolable. A floor above them, Adit watched everything with tears streaming down his cheeks.

***

Since it was a homicide, Om informed SI Manik Chand, who arrived immediately with an ambulance.

"What happened?" asked SI Manik Chand.

Om narrated whatever he had witnessed, and Grace filled in the rest. "What was her motive to do this?" asked SI Manik Chand.

Vijay, who had been silent till then, said softly, "She said she has mentioned everything in her Red Diary."

At SI Manik Chand's request, Vijay escorted him to Seema's bedroom and pointed at the Red Diary on her writing table. SI Manik Chand wore latex gloves, picked up the Red Diary and started reading loudly.

It read, "My name is Sara Mirza, and I was the daughter of Mir Mirza and Shamima Begum. My kid brother Aslam and I lived with my parents in Mirza Manzil. My father educated me well. Since I could speak fluent English, when I grew up, I got the job of a Nanny in General Oswald Truman's house. Mr Truman was a General in the British Indian Army and a very powerful man. My job was to cook and look after their autistic son, Henry Truman. Everything was going well, and there were discussions of India getting its Independence, too. On 20 February 1947, British Prime Minister Clement Attlee announced that the British would leave India by June 1948. The very next day, Mr Mohammad Ali Jinnah, the head of the Muslim League, demanded a separate Nation for the Muslims of India. The INC rejected the idea. On 3rd March 1947, Akali Dal leader Master Tara Singh notoriously made a public spectacle of his disapproval of the Pakistan demand outside the Punjab Assembly. Communal clashes erupted on 4 March after Hindus and Sikhs began demonstrations against the Pakistan demand.

"Fearing a large-scale riot, General Truman sent his wife and Henry to London. Only the General and I were left in the house. I knew the General had eyes on me, but he never made any attempts as long as his family was there. After they left, he kept calling me to his bedroom under various pretexts. One night he called me asking for water. When I went to give him water, he grabbed me. I screamed and fought back, but he tied me to the bed and raped me. From that day on, he raped me every night till I got pregnant. Afraid of my pregnancy, he plotted to kill me, but somehow, I escaped to my home. When General Truman came to know, he threatened my parents. He asked my father to get me aborted. My father refused as I was only 20 years old, and during those days, there were no good surgeons who could do abortions other than the English doctors. My father feared that the English doctor might kill me. He pleaded to him to leave us alone and we would go away to Pakistan once the migration started, but General Truman did not trust us. The very next day, the British soldiers came and set our house on fire. Then they rounded us up and started killing us one by one. They shot my dad first, then my mother and then me. After that, they picked up Aslam and threw him into the fire. I watched him scream to death. Before I died, I prayed to Allah that I come back for revenge against General Truman. Allah heard my prayer and captured my soul in the yellow bus. During the excavation, of the Rastogi's compound, my soul was released, and I found refuge in Seema's body. I will not rest till I take revenge on General Truman, who killed me and my innocent family. I will make Truman suffer a lot before killing him. I have eliminated all those who had come my way so far and have managed to put General Truman in prison. He will rot there all his life, suffer every day in jail till he is hung for his crime."

SI Manik Chand flipped a page of the Red Diary and saw a picture of Ajay Rastogi. Under his picture was written 'General Truman.'

SI Manik Chand showed Vijay the sketch and said, "Your brother was General Truman in his past life."

Vijay looked closely at the sketch, shook his head and said, "None of this makes sense. If she wanted to take revenge, she could have killed Ajay."

"Can't you see, she wants him to suffer? From the moment her spirit was released, she went after Ajay. She ruined his life in India; got him separated from me, Adit, and his own family and turned him into an alcoholic. Finally, she framed him for murder and got him on death row." Grace was shaking as she continued repeating, 'she wants him to suffer.'

"Even if I agree to all this, why did she kill the others?" asked Vijay, unable to believe the story.

"I think she killed *Dr Ratnakar* because he knew something about her. The same must have happened with *Raju Kaka*. The contractor may have been a genuine error of judgment. She killed *Abhinav* because he tried to rape Grace, and she hates rapists, and SI Majid because he was investigating her and she feared he would catch her." Said SI Manik Chand.

"It all looks possible if you put it that way," muttered Vijay, but deep inside, he wasn't convinced by the conclusion.

Chapter 12

A year had passed since Seema's death. Based on her confession statement in her Red Diary, the entire case had been closed by pinning all the murders on Seema. Rastogi Mansion had regained its old glory, the Shiv mandir had been rebuilt, and Ajay, now back, had also chosen a day job instead of doing business and was often made fun of by Grace, who had started addressing him as 'General Truman'.

Unfortunately, Adit, who was now 11 years old, never really got close to Ajay and continued to be Vijay's permanent companion in his library.

Vijay had given up the idea of getting married, and Om was too scared to experiment with another daughter-in-law again.

One day, after dinner, when Vijay, Adit and Om were sitting on the lawn, Ajay came up with a request. "Babuji, I was thinking. I will build my home separately if you can give me this land. You see, Grace and I were thinking of having our own house, but this way, not only will we have our own house, but we will be next to you as well."

Before Om could say anything, Adit reacted. "Why? Why do you want to partition this place again? You tried to do this before, and we all know what happened."

Om tried to pacify Adit, but an agitated Adit lashed out, "Don't allow this man to partition this place again, Dadu."

"Behave yourself, Adit, and say sorry to your father," said Om.

"This is not my father. He is General Truman who raped and killed Seema auntie's family," snapped Adit as he moved closer and closer to Vijay, clinging on to him.

"Stop. Stop talking about your father like this and go to your room," scolded Om.

Adit glared at Ajay and stomped off to his room. After he had left, Om looked at Ajay and said, "The child has gone through a lot of traumas, so you will have to be patient and give him time. You also have treated him very badly, so the scars will take time to heal."

"This was the reason we had thought of shifting out from here. The more Grace, Adit, and I stay together, the quicker he will bond with us. But yes, I have to be patient." Ajay walked away to his bedroom.

Om looked at Vijay and said, "I think we need some joy and happiness in this house."

Vijay looked at him and said, "Even I was thinking of that. Let me organise a mushaira evening next Saturday. I will also read some of my new poems and poems from the book I got from Jain stores. They are outstanding."

***

Saturday finally arrived, and the Rastogi Manson was completely lit up. Everyone was bussing with activity. Thirty minutes before the function, Vijay walked into the library to pick up the book from the Jain bookstore and found it missing. A worried Vijay searched everywhere but was unable to locate it. Just then, he heard a familiar knock, and Adit's voice asked, "Chachu, Me aun?"

"Please do Chote Nawab," said Vijay as he continued searching for the book of poems. Adit entered the library and asked, "Why are you looking so worried, Chachu?"

"I can't find my book of poems, and I have just twenty-five minutes left for the performance," Vijay complained.

"I can recite if you can't find the book," said Adit sweetly.

"I want to recite the fourth poem specifically, not some random poem you may have read, Adit," said Vijay as he continued searching.

Suddenly, he heard Adit reciting the very poem Vijay had in mind. Vijay turned around to see Adit sitting on the red velvet chair. He was holding the book from the Jain store but reciting without looking at it. As Vijay watched him reciting, his voice slowly changed and became manly until it reached a dual-tone voice. Around them, on the walls, the poem's lyrics started getting projected in Urdu. As a stunned Vijay sat down, mesmerised by what was happening around him, Adit walked up to him and held his hands. The moment he touched him, Vijay felt weak. He realised he could not move. Though he could see and hear everything, his entire body had been paralysed.

Adit returned to the red velvet chair, sat back, opened the book, flipped through the pages, and pulled out a picture. It was a copy of the photograph Vijay had seen earlier, but the picture was not torn this time. Vijay looked at the picture and saw a young man standing there. He was wearing a Pashtun male skirt which Vijay had assumed to be the skirt of a woman in the previous photograph.

Adit picked up the lens and held it against the face of the man in the Pashtun male skirt. Vijay looked at the face and saw his brother Ajay Rastogi staring back.

Adit saw Vijay's look of surprise and said, "Let me introduce myself; I am Adir Mirza, son of Mir Mirza and Shamima Begum.

I was born here; in this house you call Rastogi Mansion. In the 1940s, it was called Mirza Manzil." Adit tapped on the boy in the picture and said, "That's me. The bus you see here was a toy my father gave me on my first birthday." Then he tapped on Ajay's face in the picture and said, "That is my elder brother, Aslam Mirza, who is now your brother, Ajay Rastogi."

'I hated him then, and I hate him now as well. Aslam was in love with the only daughter of the British General Truman and wanted to marry her against my parents' wishes. But the girl had one condition. She would not live with my parents. Aslam asked for his share of the inheritance, but my father refused. So, he and his friends locked my parents and me in the woodshed. One of his friends raped my mother in front of me, and then they set the shed on fire. Before the flames consumed me that night, I prayed to Allah that I come back for revenge against Aslam Mirza. Allah heard my prayer and captured my soul in the yellow bus.'

'Later, even as my soul watched, Aslam and his friends buried our bodies. Aslam sold the house to General Truman and left with his girl for London. After India gained independence, the General sold the house to the Indian Government for a huge sum and joined Aslam and his daughter in London.

'To the external world, Mirza Manzil and its occupants were victims of the partition. Everyone thought the Mirza family had left for Pakistan. Nobody knew that we were buried six feet under.'

'For decades, I waited for my revenge and look at the irony: In this life, I am born to the very same couple because of whom I was killed. I was born to the very same man who killed me. Allah is great; it is his will that I am born here to exact my revenge. Aslam will die a painful death. He will die tonight while you sit here.

Once I have avenged, I will release you, and you will all become my vassals, just like Seema.'

Seeing the confused look on Vijay's face, Adit laughed and said, "Oh, I forgot to tell you. After being released during the excavation, I wondered who I should use to exact my revenge. Initially, I stayed inside Adit, but he was too small and weak. I thought of using you as you are physically strong, but then you reminded me of my father, a man of morals, ethics and values, and I did not want you to go to prison. So, I looked for someone else."

"In the meantime, you sent Adit for a check-up to Dr Ratnakar. That day was scary for me as Dr Ratnakar quickly discovered I had possessed Adit. I had to keep him quiet, so I entered Seema and killed him. I found Seema physically strong but mentally very weak. An ideal candidate for manipulation. So, I decided to use her."

"One day, I was briefing her in the library when Raju Kaka spotted me. I loved the old man, but he would have exposed me, so I was forced to kill the poor soul. Then, that stupid SI Majid Khan started suspecting Seema, so I lured him home by killing the contractor and then killed Majid by making sure he went over the railing from the top floor. I loved killing Abhinav. He reminded me of Aslam's friend who raped my mother before setting us on fire. I sneaked out and tied his shoelaces when Ajay and he argued that night. That night, I killed two birds with one stone. I killed Abhinav and got Ajay jailed. Everything would have ended there, and I would have released Seema from my hold, but then I wanted you to be free. Free so that I could have you by my side forever. So, I sacrificed Seema by getting her addicted to the bus. As I expected, you got suspicious of her, and then you know what happened. The poor thing was as innocent as a lamb. The red diary was my idea. I narrated the story which she wrote. You see, now, with her gone, all the murders have been tied to her, and there is just Grace, Om and you." Adit smiled an evil smile and whispered in Vijay's ear, "And, of course, me."

Adit looked out the window at the night sky for a few minutes and then returned to Vijay. He stood in front of him and said, 'Now that all the cases have been closed, I am free to avenge my death. Aslam killed us for the English girl. Now that I have got him out of Jail by framing everything on Seema, tonight, Aslam will burn to death in front of his wife. She should suffer just as I suffered seeing my mother burn."

Adit took a sip of water, placed the glass and a capsule next to Vijay and said, 'I stole this from the hospital. In another half an hour, you will regain your movement a little, as your nerves come back to life. When you regain some strength, have this capsule and you will be perfectly normal. But by then, I would have had my revenge. See you soon." He kissed Vijay on his cheek and walked out of the library.

***

Adit walked up the steps and searched for Ajay. He found him sitting on a wooden bench outside, hiding under the kitchen window and drinking on the sly from a steel glass. He had a cigarette in his left hand. Next to him, there was a whiskey bottle. Adit looked around and found a long ladle. He climbed on the kitchen counter, reached out of the window, and tried to push the whiskey bottle. Just then, two things happened. Grace walked out of the house to where Ajay was sitting, and Ajay tried to hide the bottle under the bench. Grace saw the bottle in Ajay's hand and snapped, "I know you have started drinking again, Ajay, so don't try to hide the bottle from me. But for now, come inside and help us. The guests will be arriving in an hour," said Grace.

Adit waited for Grace to walk away and Ajay to put the bottle back on the bench and take another swig of whiskey from his steel glass. Then he toppled the Whiskey bottle with the ladle. Hearing the sound, Ajay turned and tried to step away from the spilt whiskey. Exactly at the moment, Adit hit his wrist with the ladle. The cigarette dropped from Ajay's hand even as he looked at Adit wide-eyed and fell on the bench. Reflexively, Ajay tried to kick the cigarette off the bench with his foot, but his foot hit the bench, and it toppled. The alcohol fumes immediately caught fire and raced across the wooden bench. Before Ajay could remove his foot, his pants caught fire. It leapt to his shirt in a second, and within no time, his whole body was engulfed in flames. As his screams echoed in the quiet of the evening, Grace came running out. Seeing her husband engulfed in fire, she picked up Raju Kaka's blanket that was lying outside, dipped it in a tub of water, jumped on Ajay, and wrapped him in it. Within seconds, the wet blanket doused the flames, but Ajay was burnt very badly. Grace immediately called an ambulance, which arrived in minutes and took Ajay to a hospital.

Epilogue

Vijay came running up from the library. Oblivious to the tragedy, he asked Grace, "Where is Ajay?"

"He got burnt, and has been rushed to the hospital," she said with tears in her eyes.

"Where is Adit?" he asked.

"He is sleeping in babuji's room," she said

"Sleeping my foot," snapped Vijay as he raced to Om's room. As he entered the room, he found Adit sitting on Om's lap and watching TV. Vijay rushed towards him, yanked him off Om's lap and said, "If my brother dies, I will kill you personally."

Om pulled Adit out of Vijay's hands and asked, "What is wrong with you?"

"This evil boy set Ajay on fire. He is badly burned and has been rushed to the hospital." Snapped Vijay.

"Oh my god, will he live?" asked Om.

"I hope so, Babuji," Vijay said. Then he glared at Adit and said, "This monster left me paralysed in the library. Luckily, the effect wore off quicker than he expected. This boy is evil Babuji He used Seema to kill everyone, and now he is after Ajay."

"There is something wrong with you, Vijay; Adit has been with me for the last three hours. He was sleeping next to me. He just got up and said he wanted to watch TV. He has not left this place, so how can he paralyse you and set Ajay on fire?" asked Om.

"What? If he was here, then who was with me?" asked Vijay.

"I don't know. Maybe you are hallucinating. All I know is the child was with me," said Om.

Vijay looked at Adit, who was busy watching TV. He shook his head and walked out of the room towards his library to pick his car keys so that he could go to the hospital. As he passed the living room, he saw Grace talking to a Police officer. He overheard her saying, "I don't know, sir. He was sitting outside on the bench with a drink in one hand and a cigarette in another when I went to call him. His whiskey bottle was next to him. I don't know what happened, but as he stood up to follow me, the bench tilted, and the bottle kept on it toppled and broke. When I heard the sound and turned, I saw the cigarette drop from his hand even as he stumbled backwards. Within seconds, everything caught fire. I dipped Raju Kaka's blanket in the tub and doused the fire by wrapping him with it."

The Police officer saw Vijay and asked, "Where were you when all this happened?"

"In the library."

"And you heard nothing, saw nothing and landed just when Ajay was taken away by the ambulance. How convenient, Mr Rastogi," said the Police Officer, looking at him sternly.

Vijay gave him an angry look. He wanted to tell him about Adit, but he knew no one would believe him. "No, I did not see anything or hear anything. When I arrived, Ajay was already gone."

"You and he were not on good terms, I believe. You slapped him more than once, and he left the house because of you. He took away your business and your land. If there is one person who has a motive to kill him, it is you, Mr Rastogi," said the Police Officer.

"Vijay loved Ajay and gave away everything to him willingly. Yes, he slapped him twice, but that was because he came home drunk and misbehaved with his wife and kid," said Om, who had entered the room with Adit.

"Well, we will see after the investigation. I hope all of you will cooperate," said the Police Officer.

"Ajay is my son, his brother, this lady's husband and this boy's father. He is battling for his life in the hospital, officer. Do you think we will not cooperate?" snapped Om.

After the cop left, Vijay turned to Om and said, "I can't believe he suspects me."

"What is so wrong with it? Even you suspected an innocent child," said Om, holding Adit closely.

"But I spoke to him Babuji. He told me how it all happened," argued Vijay.

Listening to the conversation, Grace walked up to Vijay and said, "You were fast asleep in the library when I entered looking for Ajay there. That was five minutes before I spoke to Ajay outside. You must have had a nightmare, Vijay. All these months have been traumatic for all of us. Even I see and hear things in my sleep."

"You mean to say the long conversation Adit had with me, the way he paralysed me and told me how each person was killed, was all a dream?" asked Vijay

"We don't know what you dreamt or heard, Vijay. All we know is what we saw. Grace saw the accident, and Adit was with me the whole time, and you were sleeping in your library," said Om.

Vijay shook his head and started muttering as he returned to the library. "Am I going mad? Do I see things?" he kept asking himself as he walked to the library.

Behind him, Grace and Om looked at each other with glazed eyes. Then they looked at Adit. He gave them a wicked smile - 'He had control over them now.' Om and Grace smiled back, bowed and walked away.

***

It was half-past eleven that night, and Vijay, after returning from the hospital, was drowning his sorrows in a bottle of vodka as the doctors had given up on Ajay and told him it was just a matter of time before he died.. He was at least five drinks down when he heard the familiar knock on the door. An innocent, sweet voice asked, "Chachu, *mai aun*?"

Shankara

Inspired by the bouncers of Asola-Fatehpur Beri in Haryana, Shankara is the story of an innocent, good-hearted young man from Haryana who cherished a simple dream of becoming a bodyguard for a renowned singer. But fate had other things in store for him. Little did he know that the path to his dream would be bloody and violent.

Prologue

Morni was a village in the Panchkula district of Haryana. The town sat on the mountainside, at 4,000 ft above sea level, and was known for its Himalayan views, flora, and lakes. Located forty-five kilometres from the capital city of Chandigarh, Morni derived its name from a just and noble queen who once ruled the area two thousand years ago. While the mountains were covered with Pine trees, the plains below were covered with acres of agricultural farmlands.

The majority of the farmlands in Morni were owned by two prominent Jat Zamindars, Rana Singh Jat and Ram Singh Jat. Though they were distantly related, they did not see eye to eye. They were born into families that had generational dislikes for each other. They fought constantly over trivial issues because both, like their ancestors, were highly egoistic and hell-bent on proving themselves to each other.

Chapter 1

Rana was married to a local, illiterate Jat girl named Pritam. Pritam came from a farming family in Haryana and was the daughter of a friend of Rana's father. Unfortunately, Pritam could not bear children because Rana had a weak sperm count. So, they adopted his nephew Uttam Singh Jat as their son. Rana's infertility was a point of ridicule in both families and added fuel to the already raging fire between Rana and Ram.

Determined to outshine Rana, Ram found himself a beautiful, educated woman from Kerala named Rukmini. Born in Eramal, a small village in Kerala, Rukmini journeyed 3,000 km north after her marriage to start a new life in the hills of Morni with Ram Singh. Rukmini gave birth to a boy whom they named Veer Singh Jat. However, being half South Indian, locals gave him a nickname—Anna Singh Jat. Rukmini and Ram also loved that name and addressed him as Anna.

Like their fathers, Anna and Uttam grew up hating each other. After Rana and Ram's deaths, their enmity spilt into the open. Both often quarrelled over land acquisition. To add to Uttam's misery, Anna teased him in public, by calling him an adopted child. This angered Uttam more than anything which led to physical fights between the cousins.

Though from the same caste as Rana and Ram, the smaller and poorer Jat farmers were forced to work for the duo as salaried employees since their lands had been mortgaged to Anna and Uttam's families for decades. When Uttam and Anna reached a marriageable age, their mothers began searching for suitable brides. Uttam married a girl named Harpreet from Chandigarh. Anna wanted to marry Manpreet, a local farmer's daughter with whom he was in love, but Rukmini refused. "If you want to be superior to Uttam in Morni, you must win elections and become an MLA. To win elections, you need lots of money—more money than you have currently. And that will come only if you get married into a wealthy family," she said.

Anna dumped Manpreet and married a Sikh named Jasleen as per his mother's advice. Jasleen was the only child of wealthy parents, who showered Anna with gold and cash as a dowry. With his newfound wealth, Anna spent the next five years acquiring land and expanding his influence in Haryana.

***

Sukhdev Singh Jat was a small Jat farmer whose land had been mortgaged to Anna's family for three generations. Sukhdev's father was Ram Singh's bodyguard. Though Anna and Sukhdev went to the same school and were childhood friends, when they grew up, tradition took over, and Anna made Sukhdev his bodyguard. Though it was humiliating, Sukhdev kept quiet and did his duty diligently as he had no choice.

As youngsters, Anna and Sukhdev both had a crush on Manpreet, but she loved Anna. For her, Sukhdev was a dear friend. When Anna dumped Manpreet for Jasleen, she was heartbroken and devastated, but Sukhdev filled the vacuum. When he proposed to her, she agreed, and they got married. This irked Anna a lot, as he never thought the woman he loved would get married to his bodyguard. Whenever he got a chance, he humiliated Sukhdev, but Sukhdev took it on his chin to avoid any argument.

A couple of years later, Uttam's wife, Harpreet, gave birth to a boy named Akhilesh. Not to be left behind, Anna's wife, Jasleen had twins a month later: a boy named Vijay and a girl named Gauri. A few months earlier, Sukhdev's wife, Manpreet, had already delivered two boys, Kishan & Shankar. All the children went to the same school and grew up together.

When Vijay and Gauri were six years old, Jasleen was diagnosed with a rare, incurable cancer. Anna tried his level best to get her treated by the best doctors in New Delhi but failed. Six months later Jasleen died, leaving behind Anna and the twins. Anna found managing his work and the twins challenging and contemplated marrying again. However, his mother, Rukmini, intervened again and advised, "Stay a widower and project yourself as a one-woman man and a doting father to your twins. It will help you in politics."

"With no wife and a huge empire to handle, how can I take care of the kids alone?" asked Anna.

"I will take care of Vijay & Gauri. You start building a strong foundation for your political journey." Rukmini said.

Once again, Anna followed his mother's advice. As predicted by Rukmini, within a year, Anna had a vast fan base in Morni. Seeing him get popular, Uttam also started wooing people towards him with financial support and freebies.

As the years went by, all the children grew into adults. A studious Gauri completed her education and became a doctor. She set up a small clinic and served the people of Morni, earning everyone's love and respect. But Vijay was just the opposite. He dropped out of school and gallivanted the whole day with his friends. People in Morni hated him. If he was not drinking or gambling, he would be driving around in his open jeep with his friends, teasing the local women.

If there was one thing Rukmini felt she had failed at, it was the bringing up of Vijay. Vijay was a spoiled brat with all the vices, including womanising. While Vijay was busy with his nefarious activities, it was Gauri that Anna looked up to handle the business when he was out of town for his political work. As Anna got more and more involved in politics, Gauri started managing his large empire because Vijay showed no interest in working. Soon, word spread that Gauri would be Anna's successor.

Uttam's son Akhilesh also turned out to be a disappointment. Born wealthy, he also dropped out of school, got into drugs and ended up as a liability to his family and the village. But being their only child, Uttam & Harpreet pampered him. Akhilesh and Vijay had competing gangs, and each tried to outdo the other constantly.

***

Chapter 2

Sukhdev's sons had a similar history but with a small twist. Kishan, the eldest son, was academically strong, and after finishing school, he cleared the IPS exams and became a Police Officer posted in a place called Kunnar. The younger son, Shankara, hated studies.

Sukhdev wanted Shankara to be a District Collector and went about telling everyone about his dream to the extent that Morni nicknamed Shankara the *'Collector'*. But much to Sukhdev's lousy luck, Shankara stopped attending school after his 12th year. He spent all his time in the gym building his body. When Sukhdev asked him about his plans, he said he wanted to be a bodyguard like Sukhdev. Disappointed that instead of being a collector, his son wanted to be a 'slave' to someone, Sukhdev scolded Shankara constantly, so he stayed out of the house most of the time.

Though his mother, Manpreet, pampered him and always came to his rescue, Shankara's true love was his childhood friend, Kusum Kalra, the daughter of his neighbours, Prem and Kiran Kalra. Kusum worked at the local post office as a Lower Division Clerk. But being a government job, she got a good salary and all government benefits. Her parents, Prem and Kiran, were nurses in the local Government hospital and close friends of Sukhdev and Manpreet. Shankara and Kusum's love affair began when they were kids; Manpreet teased Shankara as a child that Kusum would be his future wife, and a thrilled Shankara took it upon himself to always protect Kusum. Over the years, the two got close, and love blossomed. Both mothers knew about their love for each other and silently hoped the love would culminate into a formal relationship. But scared of their husbands, they kept it a secret.

Kusum loved Shankara with all his flaws because she knew he was an honest, God-fearing young man who loved her deeply, even though all the girls in Morni craved him. Shankara's elder brother, Kishan, loved Anna's daughter, Gauri, but was scared to express his love. Little did he know that Gauri was secretly in love with Shankara and was facing the same difficulty as him, of expressing her love. Posted in Kunnar, Kishan did not get a chance to be in Morni. He came on his annual leave once a year but never gathered the courage to speak with Gauri.

In Anna and Uttam's family, the sons failed their fathers, and both Akhilesh and Vijay became rogues. They treated Sukhdev's sons like their slaves. While Kishan escaped the humiliation as he was posted in Kunnar, Shankara had to endure the brunt of their ridicule. But unlike Kishan, Shankara was not the type who would take bad behaviour from anyone, especially Akhilesh and Vijay and would often get into fights with them. They would get beaten up by Shankara and complain to their fathers, who would then complain to Sukhdev. Sukhdev took out his frustrations on Shankara by punishing him, even though he knew his son was not wrong.

Every time Sukhdev beat Shankara over a dispute with Akhilesh and Vijay, he would put medicine on the welts in repentance. Shankara knew his father loved him, and it was the bottled-up frustration within him that was coming out.

***

Kishan was in charge of a Kunnar Police Station in Rohtak. Kunnar was famous for regular encounters between the Police and gangsters. The Police personnel in Kunnar were tough and followed the 'Shoot first, then talk' principle, which was against Kishan's philosophy. When he took over, he tried to change his team's thinking but ended up reluctantly joining them instead of changing their habits.

Seeing the rogue atmosphere in Kunnar, Sukhdev feared for Kishan's safety. With Kishan not applying for a transfer, Sukhdev took it upon himself to get Kishan back to Morni. One day he asked Anna, "You are such a big Politician now, everyone knows you in Morni and Chandigarh. You are well-networked and connected, even with the Chief Minister. Can you please help Kishan get a transfer to Morni?"

Anna agreed, but he told him it would cost Rs 25 lakhs to bribe the Police Commissioner. When Sukhdev told Anna that he did not have the money. He said, "Mortgage your house to me and I will pay the money on your behalf." Sukhdev spoke with Manpreet and they decided to mortgage their house to Anna without the children's knowledge. Now, not only their land, but their house was also under Anna's control. Within a month, Kishan was transferred to Morni. Assuming it was a regular transfer, Kishan was thrilled and quickly made plans to win over Gauri.

A month later, when Shankara bumped into Vijay, he taunted him and said, "You beat me last time, but from now onwards, you won't be able to do anything."

"Why?" asked Shankara.

"Because now your house is also in my control. Raise your voice, and I will throw you all out on the streets," said Vijay, roaring off in his jeep. That night, over dinner, when Shankara and Kishan raised the topic, Sukhdev and Manpreet confessed and told them what had happened.

"So, I am starting my career as the SHO in Morni with a Rs 3 lakh debt per month? My monthly salary is only half of that! But it's okay. I will pay it off in two years, including the interest," said Kishan.

"We will eat less, but we will save and pay back from my salary, too," said Sukhdev. Then he looked at Shankara and said, "At least now find a job for yourself."

***

Chapter 3

Unlike Kishan, who was a simpleton, Shankara was a flamboyant daredevil, unafraid to take on anything and anybody. If he saw someone doing something unethical or wrong in Morni, he would call them out. Whenever the villagers needed help against Vijay or Akhilesh's goons, they would call Shankara. For justice in Morni, no one went to Kishan or the Police station; they all went to Shankara, the 'Collector'.

Sometimes, Shankara's justice would end up in a fight, where he would beat up his opponent so badly that he would be hauled to the police station. Then Kishan would have to intervene and request his subordinates to release Shankara. Though Shankara felt that he had become a liability in the house without a job, Kishen loved his brother a little too much to let him suffer. So, he would finance him quietly whenever Shankara needed money for his outings.

Apart from Kusum, Shankara had a very dear friend called Pawan Singh, a frail young man, a year younger than him. Pawan idolised Shankara and was always stuck to him like a leech. Kusum, Shankara and Pawan were a team and very close. They spent all their free time together watching movies, listening to their favourite singer, Prem Dhillon, and going for joy rides on Kusum's 'Hero Honda' scooter. Every time the trio passed by the police station, the constable on duty would tell Kishan, "We saw your brother again riding a three-seater without a helmet." In turn,

Kishan would jokingly say, "If I put him in jail who will fight your case on the street?".

Crazy after Prem Dhillon and his songs, Shankara, Pawan, and Kusum knew the lyrics of all his songs.

Once they learned that Dhillon was coming to Morni for a video shoot, and Kishan was providing the security. Shankara requested Kishan, "Brother, please introduce us to Dhillon, no?"

Kishan smiled at Shankara's childish request and said, "I will see what I can do."

The next day, when Sukhdev saw Shankara dressing up, he asked, "Where are you going now?"

"To meet Prem Dhillo! Kishan Bhaiyya said he will arrange it, and I am confident of his capabilities," said Shankara with a big smile.

"I know he can get you an introduction with Prem Dhillon, but when will you start showing your abilities?" mocked Sukhdev.

"I am capable. I do all the work around the house, run errands, and take care of you and Mom," said Shankara, powdering his face.

"The only thing you're capable of doing is gallivanting and wasting your brother's money. You know very well he is saving up to pay back Anna. Why can't you get a proper job and contribute to the house expenses?" asked Sukhdev.

"Just wait, Baba. One day, I will buy you a house bigger than Anna's," said Shankara as he combed his hair.

Sukhdev was about to respond sarcastically when someone knocked on the door. When Sukhdev opened it, he saw one of Anna's men standing outside. Behind him, Anna waved out to Sukhdev from his jeep. "Come with us. We have to meet a farmer who is refusing to sell his land."

Sukhdev nodded and began following the man. He took two steps, then returned to Shankara, and said, "Don't buy me a house bigger than Anna's. If you can even buy me a pair of Ray-Ban sunglass like Anna's, I will be happy." Then he turned and walked towards Anna's jeep.

Behind him, Shankara said, "Baba, why buy a Ray-Ban glass like Anna's? One day I will get you Anna's very own Ray-Bans."

Sukhdev rolled his eyes, shook his head and entered the jeep with Anna.

That evening, at Dhillon's shooting site, during a break, Kishan took the trio to Dhillon and said, "Dhillon Bhai, this is my brother Shankara and his friends, Kusum and Pawan. They are your fans and are here for your autograph. Please don't disappoint them."

Dhillon smiled at them, took a book and pen from Shankara and started writing their names and signing against them with a small note for each of them.

As the shoot continued, Shankara noticed Dhillon's tough-looking bodyguards with side arms, standing a few feet away from him, scanning the crowd. Impressed by the bodyguards, at that instant, Shankara decided on his future; "I will become Dhillon's bodyguard one day."

Chapter 4

One day when Kusum was in the market with Pawan to buy vegetables, Vijay laid his eyes on her. He looked at her for a few minutes and then declared to his friend, "Tonight I will bed Kusum." Having said that, he got out of his jeep, walked over to where she was standing and said, "I will pay darling."

"There is no need. I have money," said Kusum. As she opened her purse to take out the money, Vijay grabbed her left hand.

"I said I will pay," he insisted.

"Leave my hand."

"What if I don't?" asked Vijay.

In response, Kusum glared at him and before he could know it she swung her right hand, slapped him hard across his face. The cracking sound of the slap made heads turn. A humiliated Vijay let go of her hand and tried to rip Kusum's shirt off, but the only thing Vijay could grab was her scarf. As she stepped back further, Pawan quickly called Shankara. "Vijay is trying to harass Kusum in the market. He tried to rip her shirt off, luckily, she stepped back, but he managed to pull off her scarf. He is still going after her. Come fast."

Shankara was in the next lane, getting his bike serviced. When he got Pawan's call, he started the bike and raced towards Vijay. In a matter of minutes, he was in the vegetable market. Seeing Shankara, everyone started shouting, 'Collector has come'. Hearing the commotion, Vijay turned and saw Shankara.

Shankara had arrived just in time to see Vijay attempting to molest Kusum. His heart pounded with a mixture of rage and determination. Without wasting a moment, he parked his bike and advanced toward Vijay, his eyes blazing with fury. Each step he took was filled with resolve, and he was ready to protect Kusum and confront Vijay, who had dropped the scarf and now stood facing Shankara.

Shankara clenched his fists as he strode towards Vijay. The scene before him fuelled his anger, and the determination to protect Kusum surged through his veins. Sensing the impending confrontation, Vijay pushed Kusum aside and turned to face Shankara with a smug grin, confident of his strength.

As Shankara approached, Pawan set his phone's timer for 8 minutes and said, "The 8-minute timer is on."

A bystander who overheard asked, "Why 8 minutes?"

"He is Shankara, Shiva's avatar on earth, and 8 is Shiva's number. It represents infinity. Shankara has infinite strength."

Shankara wasted no time. With a swift motion, he launched a powerful punch at Vijay's face. Vijay staggered back, clearly taken aback by the force of the blow. Regaining his balance, Vijay retaliated with a vicious kick to Shankara's midsection, but Shankara anticipated the move, sidestepping just in time. The two circled each other, eyes locked, the tension thick in the air. Vijay lunged forward, throwing a series of rapid punches. Shankara deftly blocked and countered with a well-placed elbow to Vijay's ribs. The impact caused Vijay to gasp in pain, clutching his side.

But Vijay was not one to back down easily. With a roar of anger, he charged at Shankara, attempting to tackle him to the ground. Shankara, however, used Vijay's momentum against him, flipping him over and sending him crashing to the pavement. The sound of the impact echoed through the market.

Breathing heavily, Shankara moved in to finish the fight. He delivered a powerful kick to Vijay's chest, knocking the wind out of him. Vijay coughed and spluttered, struggling to rise, but Shankara was relentless. He reached out, grabbed Vijay's right hand and snapped it at the elbow, saying, "This is for touching her."

Vijay screamed in pain, but Shankara grabbed him by the collar and lifted him slightly off the ground. "This is for Kusum," Shankara growled before delivering a final, bone-rattling punch that sent Vijay sprawling, unconscious.

Shankara stood over Vijay's limp form, his breath coming in ragged gasps. He turned to Kusum, who had been watching the fight with wide eyes and said, "Come here."

Her fear melted into relief as she ran to Shankara, embracing him tightly. "It's over," Shankara whispered, holding her close. "You're safe now."

As the crowd roared, "Collector, Collector," Shankara looked at Pawan and raised an eyebrow. Pawan gave a thumbs-up sign and said, "Exactly 8 minutes."

***

When Anna learned that Vijay had been rushed to Gauri's clinic with a fractured elbow and bruises, he was furious. He rushed to see his son. Sukhdev was with him when he reached the clinic and found out what had happened.

"How many times have I told you to stay quiet till I win the elections? Your stupid activities are not helping me in my campaign, you idiot." Anna shouted at Vijay.

Then he turned to Sukhdev and said, "This is a matter of prestige now, Sukhi. I will accept nothing less than a public apology from Shankara. He has to apologise to Vijay at the same place he beat him up, in front of everyone."

When Sukhdev instructed Shankara to apologise publicly, being an obedient son, Shankara agreed. Three days later when Vijay arrived in the market after getting discharged from the clinic, Shankara apologised to Vijay in front of everyone. "I am sorry for having beaten you blue-black and breaking your elbow." He said loudly.

However, a wily Vijay did not accept the apology. "I want Sukhdev to touch my feet and apologise," said Vijay.

As the crowd looked on, Sukhdev turned towards Anna, who nodded. Swallowing his pride, he moved forward to touch Vijay's feet, but Shankara did not allow it. Instead, he pushed Sukhdev away and kicked Vijay's ankle. The decisive blow broke Vijay's ankle.

As the crowd looked on in stunned silence, Anna roared and lifted his revolver to shoot Shankara but stopped when he heard his mother's voice behind him. "Put the gun back, Anna," shouted Rukmini, who had arrived on the scene with Gauri.

Anna continued training his gun on Shankara for a full minute before holstering it. Then he nodded to Sukhdev and left in his jeep.

Back home, while Rukmini pacified Anna, he was livid. "I should have shot him right there," he hissed.

"And you would have gone to jail. Use your head and not the heart. The elections are coming up in six months. Do you want to be there to fight the elections or count the bars in Chandigarh?" she asked. Seeing Anna controlling his temper, Rukmini held his hand and said softly, "I plan to convert this to our advantage."

"How? He broke Vijay's elbow and ankle, and you are asking me to keep quiet?"

"No. I am asking you to take advantage of the situation. Let's face it: unfortunately, Vijay is a no-good spoiled brat. He is arrogant. He assumes he will someday own your empire because he is your son. Besides being your blood, he has no qualities to run your empire. In reality, all the administration is handled by Gauri. Can you look me in the eye and tell me Vijay is fit to take over after you?" asked Rukmini.

Anna lowered his eyes and shook his head, "No. He will bring everything to the ground in a week. But he is my son. How can I forget him?"

"Even if you know he is a liability to your future? Forget him and focus on adding to your strength. You will be contesting for the MLA position in a few months. You have worked hard for this all your life, and your son is spoiling it with his alcoholism and womanising. I have a better idea." Rukmini said.

"What is it?" asked Anna.

"Get Gauri married to Shankar," said Rukmini.

"What? You want me to get my daughter married to my bodyguard's son? Never." Anna was shocked at the suggestion.

"Think with your head and not with your heart, Anna. This empire needs a strong successor. Shankara is strong, daring, feared and loved by all. He will demolish Uttam and his family. Sukhdev is financially weak, but he comes from the same caste and faith as us. In Haryana, people listen to their hearts, not their heads, as we do in Kerala. Imagine the public reaction when they hear that the benevolent Anna stood on the side of Dharma. He is the protector of women. He got his daughter married to a simple boy from a simple family. Morni will say that a generous Anna embraced his friend and converted the friendship into a relationship. They will say that Anna gave more weight to friendship than to economic status. Anna is a great and generous man. We want him to be an MLA because he is just and fair… Can you hear Morni screaming your name with respect, Anna?" asked Rukmini.

Anna closed his eyes and visualized the scene of him entering the Vigyan Bhavan for the swearing-in with people screaming, 'Anna, Anna' all around him. Gauri and Shankar were next to him, too… Anna opened his eyes, looked at Rukmini softly, and asked, "Will Gauri agree?"

Rukmini surprised him with her response. "Gauri has been in love with Shankara since she was in school."

Chapter 5

When Anna called Gauri and asked her if she would marry Shankara, she shyly nodded in agreement and ran back to her room. A thrilled Anna called Sukhdev.

When Sukhdev arrived, he looked worried. "I am sorry for what Shankara did to Vijay Baba. You can deduct the money from my salary for his medical expenses Annaji. And when I go home, I will punish Shankara," said Sukhdev.

Anna held Sukhdev by his shoulders and said, "This is not a moment for apologies and sadness, Sukhi. This is a moment of joy. Look, Vijay got what he deserved. If I was in Shankara's place, even I would have done the same if a woman was being molested. I called you for something else. My daughter Gauri loves Shankara, and I want to get them married. I want Shankara to be my successor. Please don't say no."

After the initial shock, Sukhdev was overwhelmed with happiness. He broke down and cried on Anna's shoulder. "You are truly a generous man, Annaji. I never knew you harboured so much love and affection for Shankara and my family. Yes, I agree to the proposal. I will go home in the evening and inform Shankara and Manpreet."

Anna hugged Sukhdev as Rukmini watched them from a corner, smiling. That evening, an overjoyed Anna called a Panchayat of the elders in the village and announced the wedding of Gauri and Shankara. The news spread like wildfire and reached Pawan's ears, who panicked and ran to inform Shankar and Kusum.

When Sukhdev broke the news to Manpreet back home, Prem and Kiran were with her. While Prem was happy for Shankara, Manpreet and Kiran were upset. When questioned about their anger, they revealed the secret. "Our children have been in love with each other since they were in school," they told their husbands.

"But I gave Anna my word, and Anna announced it in the village panchayat," said Sukhdev

"But Shankara and Kusum have loved each other since childhood. They were betrothed to each other when they were five years old. Manpreet gave me her word," argued Kiran.

"What will we do?" asked Prem.

"If Manpreet has given her word to you, then I cannot break it," said Sukhdev.

"The same goes for me," said Prem.

"But you have given your word to Annaji, too. Gauri is dreaming of marrying me, Baba," said Shankara, who had just entered with Kusum and Pawan.

"What do we do?" asked Pawan.

"There is only one way," said Sukhdev.

"What is it?" asked Kusum.

"Both of you should run away from this place tonight. Pack your bags and leave," said Sukhdev.

"No, Baba. I can't leave you all to suffer at the hands of Anna and his goons," countered Shankara.

"You forget about us. I will manage Anna. You two leave tonight under the cover of darkness. Go to Chandigarh and then take the early morning train to Mumbai. My good friend Sultan Ali Khan lives there. I will inform him, and he will take care of you. Sultan is very resourceful and will find you a job as well. You will be safe with him. But leave tonight," said Sukhdev.

Teary-eyed and reluctant, Shankara and Kusum left Morni that night. Pawan, booked their tickets and dropped them off at the Chandigarh railways station on Kusum's Scooter. Three hours later, the young couple boarded the train to Mumbai.

When Sukhdev told Anna the following day that Shankara had fled Morni with Kusum, Vijay seethed with rage. A devastated Gauri broke down before Rukmini, saying, "Dadi, I have no wish to live now."

Seeing his daughter sad, Anna screamed in anger and threatened Sukhdev. "Shankara has ruined my name in the village, but I can handle that. But he broke Gauri's heart, and for that, I will not forgive him. I will drag him out of whichever hole he hides in and make him suffer for this. I will make sure Kusum sits as a prostitute in the Kothas of Morni, and you, Sukhdev, will watch their ruin. That will be your punishment," shouted Anna.

Vijay, who witnessed everything, turned and walked out of the room. Seeing him leave, Rukmini knew Vijay would retaliate.

"Rein in that mad Vijay. He will ruin your future as an MLA. Let bygones be bygones. Focus on your elections; we can use the sympathy to get votes," advised Rukmini

"What kind of mother are you? Your son's name is ruined, your granddaughter's life is ruined, and you are worried about my election? Shame on you, mother. I have always listened to you but now I will listen to my heart. I will not stop Vijay. He will find Shankara and bring him to me," said Anna, storming out of the house.

Realising that this was turning into a small-scale war, Gauri called Kishan. "My mad brother is coming to your house to take revenge. Protect your family."

When Kishan learned about Vijay's arrival, he posted a few policemen around Prem and Sukhdev's houses, but they were no match for Anna's goons.

Led by Vijay, the goons thrashed the policemen, entered the house, and manhandled Kiran and Manpreet. When Sukhdev and Prem intervened, they were beaten up as well. Unable to withstand the torture, Prem confessed to Vijay that Shankara and Kusum had fled to Mumbai, but he did not give the details of their whereabouts, claiming he did not know. "I am sure they have fled to Mumbai, but I don't know where."

Even after a month of relentless searching, Vijay couldn't track down Shankara or Kusum. The frustration weighed on him like a heavy cloud, and he was on the verge of abandoning the chase. Just as hope began to slip away, one of his friends approached him with a new idea. "If we shadow Pawan," he said quietly, "it's only a matter of time before he leads us straight to Shankara."

Vijay's heart raced. A flicker of hope reignited—one last chance.

Meanwhile, when Shankara and Kusum reached Mumbai, they were received by Sultan Ali Khan's men and taken to his house. Sultan ran a martial arts school next to his house in Mahim. Ali Khan told Shankara that he and Sukhdev were very good friends.

After listening to Shankara and Kusum's story, Ali Khan pacified them. "This is Mumbai. Finding people and jobs here is difficult, unless you are connected. Sleep without fear tonight. Tomorrow, I will take you to a friend of mine and see if he can find you a job," he said.

The following day, after breakfast, Ali Khan took Shankara to meet his friend. To Shankara's surprise, the friend was none other than singer Dhillon. Seeing him again, Shankara forgot protocol and hugged him tightly. "Do you remember me? You gave me an autograph in Morni, remember?" gushed Shankara.

Seeing Dhillon's confused look, Ali Khan stepped in and said, "The lad is excited after meeting you. He is my friend Sukhdev's son. He has landed himself in a spot of trouble."

"Tell me what help you need, Ali Khan. You know I am always indebted to you." Dhillon had very high regard for Ali Khan, as he had saved Dhillon's life a few years ago.

Ali Khan explained Shankara's issue in detail: "He cannot stay with me forever, and he needs a job to survive in Mumbai."

"Is he a martial arts expert?" asked Dhillon

"No. But he can *really* fight," said Ali Khan.

"In that case, let him join my team of bodyguards. I have three, he can be the fourth," said Dhillon.

Shankara was thrilled that his dream had come true. He thanked Lord Shiva for the miracle and returned home with Ali Khan. On the way back, he asked Ali Khan, "What's the story between you two?"

"It's an old story," said Ali Khan.

"It is a long ride home and I love listening to stories," said Shankara.

Chapter 6

(Flashback)

When Dhillon's stars began to rise as a Bollywood singer, and he moved to Mumbai, the city of dreams, his success cast a shadow on one man—Boxer Juggy. The son of the notorious Mafia Don, Salim Kutta. With Dhillon's success, Juggy's insecurities flared. Unable to stomach Dhillon's growing fame, Juggy complained to his father. Salim, never one to tolerate a threat to his family's pride, made a cold decision—Dhillon had to be silenced, once and for all.

One evening Salim sent some goons to Dhillon's house in Mahim to finish him. Not finding him there, the goons questioned the neighbours, who told them that Dhillon was jogging at Worli Beach. The goons set off for Worli Beach carrying knives and choppers. After searching for a while, they spotted Dhillon jogging by the water and immediately began chasing him.

Ali Khan was enjoying a peaceful stroll along the beach, the waves gently lapping at the shore, when a commotion caught his attention. In the distance, he saw a group of goons wielding knives and machetes, chasing the terrified singer Dhillon in a jeep. Dhillon's desperate cries for help echoed across the sand as he sprinted for his life.

Without a moment's hesitation, Ali Khan sprang into action. He sprinted towards the chaos, his muscles tensing, ready for battle.

As the jeep screeched to a halt, the goons leapt out, brandishing their weapons with menacing intent. Ali Khan intercepted them, placing himself between the goons and the fleeing Dhillon. The group leader, a burly man with a scar across his cheek, sneered at Ali Khan. "You picked the wrong day to be a hero," he snarled, raising his machete. Ali Khan didn't even flinch. Instead, he darted forward, his fist connecting with the leader's jaw in a lightning-fast uppercut. The man staggered back, stunned, as Ali Khan whirled to face the remaining five goons.

The beach became a battlefield. One lunged at Ali Khan with a knife, but Ali deftly sidestepped, grabbing the man's arm and twisting it until the knife clattered to the ground. With a swift kick, he sent the goon sprawling into the sand. Another goon swung a machete at Ali Khan, but Ali ducked under the blade and countered with a powerful elbow strike to the man's ribs, followed by a knee to the stomach. The goon doubled over in pain, dropping his weapon. Two more rushed at Ali Khan simultaneously. He grabbed a fallen knife from the sand and parried their attacks, moving with precision and speed. He disarmed one of them with a quick slash to the wrist and knocked him out with a punch to the temple. The other received a spinning kick to the chest, sending him flying backwards. The final goon, seeing his comrades defeated, hesitated. Ali Khan used this moment of hesitation to his advantage. He charged forward, delivering a series of rapid punches that left the goon dazed and disoriented. With a final, powerful kick, he sent the last goon crashing to the ground.

Breathing heavily, Ali Khan stood amidst the fallen goons, his eyes scanning the beach for any remaining threats. Dhillon, now safe, approached cautiously, his face a mix of relief and awe. "Thank you," he said, his voice trembling. "You saved my life."

Ali Khan nodded; his expression serious but calm. "I'm just doing what's right," he replied. "Let's get you somewhere safe."

Later, when Ali Khan dropped him home, Dhillon hugged Ali Khan and said, "I will never forget you. I am indebted to you for life."

True to his word, Dhillon kept in touch with Ali Khan even after becoming a national celebrity.

Chapter 7

When Shankara left for work the next day, Ali Khan said, "Take care of Dhillon as you would of Kusum, and uphold my reputation, son." Shankara promised to safeguard Dhillon with his life and worked hard and diligently to establish Dhillon's trust in him. He made sure everything Dhillon needed was available without him having to ask for it. As the months rolled by, Dhillon and Shankara became close.

One day, when Dhillon and his girlfriend were shopping at a jewellery store, Salim Kutta's goons barged into the shop looking for him. The shop owner asked Dhillon and his girlfriend to hide on the first floor. When the goons could not find Dhillon, they took all the customers hostage and asked the shopkeeper where Dhillon was hiding. "If you don't give us Dhillon in the next five minutes, we will start shooting the hostages," said the group leader, pointing to the man carrying a gun.

That day, Dhillon's three bodyguards were with him in the store, but instead of protecting him, they acted as if they were customers and became hostages. Shankara was waiting in the car when he saw the goons downing the shutters. He tried to contact the bodyguards inside, but the body guards had switched off their phones.

Suspecting foul play, Shankara exited the car, went around the shop, slipped through the toilet ventilator and landed silently on the cold, tiled floor of the jewellery shop's rear room. His eyes quickly adjusted to the dim light, as he heard the muffled voices of the goons in the main area. Moving with cat-like stealth, he peered around the corner and saw four armed men. Three had knives, and one—a gun.

A tall man with a scar running down his cheek, who was keeping the hostages in check, had his gun pointed menacingly towards the customers. The other three were searching the shop, heading towards the stairs that led to the first floor, where Dhillon and his girlfriend were hiding. Shankara knew he had to act fast. He picked up a small, heavy statue from a nearby shelf and hurled it at the goon guarding the hostages. The statue struck the man's head with a dull thud, and he crumpled to the floor, unconscious.

The noise drew the attention of the other three goons. They turned and saw Shankara standing defiantly, ready for a fight. One of them, a stocky man with a shaved head, suddenly pulled out a gun from a black bag he was carrying, but Shankara was quicker. He sprinted forward, grabbing the gun barrel, twisting it from the goon's grip and then knocking him out cold with a swift, brutal punch to the face. The remaining two goons exchanged a nervous glance before charging at Shankara simultaneously. One aimed a wild punch, but Shankara ducked, his reflexes honed from years of street fighting. He retaliated with a knee to the man's gut, followed by an elbow to the back of his head, sending him sprawling to the ground.

The last goon, a wiry man with a sneer permanently etched on his face, pulled out a knife and lunged at Shankara. The blade glinted in the dim light as it sliced through the air. Shankara dodged the initial attack, then grabbed the goon's wrist, twisting it until the knife clattered to the floor. With a quick, fluid motion, he delivered a spinning kick to the goon's chest, knocking the wind out of him and sending him crashing into a display case. Within minutes, everything was over. The shop fell silent, except for the heavy breathing of the hostages and the distant sound of sirens approaching, thanks to a neighbour who had called the cops.

Shankara scanned the room, ensuring all the goons were incapacitated. Satisfied, he made his way upstairs to find Dhillon and his girlfriend. On the first floor, Shankara found them huddled in a corner. The girl's eyes were wide with fear. He extended a hand, helping them to their feet. "It's over," he said calmly. Dhillon and his girlfriend exchanged relieved glances before following Shankara downstairs.

As they emerged from the shop, the police arrived, taking the unconscious goons into custody. As Dhillon embraced his girlfriend tightly, Shankara watched the bodyguards coming out with the hostages. He walked up to the Inspector. "Do you see those three bodybuilders along with the hostages?" he asked.

"Yes, what about them?" asked the Inspector.

"They are supposed to be Dhillon's bodyguards, but all three are on Salim Kutta's payroll. Instead of protecting Dhillon, they let the goons take control," he explained.

"Arrest those three and put them in the jeep," said the inspector, pointing at the bodyguards. As the policemen closed on them, the bodyguards tried to escape, but they were quickly, apprehended and cuffed.

"Why did you do that?" asked Dhillon.

"While I was tackling the goons, I saw that all three of your bodyguards had their guns in their holsters. They could have neutralised the goons, but they chose not to. They were accomplices in this hostage drama," replied Shankara.

Dhillon looked at Shankara and said, "From this day forward, you are the head of my security. Make a loyal team under you and travel with me."

Shankara's new title came with a massive hike in salary. That evening, after dinner Shankara told Ali Khan, "Sultan Bhai, you have looked after us all these months, but now I have a good job and a great salary. I think it is time for Kusum and I to move into our house and get married."

Ali Khan shook his head and said, "No. First, get married and then move into a new house."

Chapter 8

(Present)

A week later, two things happened. One, CCTV footage of the failed jewellery shop heist went viral and got Vijay's attention. Two, Pawan got a call from Shankara, asking him to come to Mumbai as a witness for his and Kusum's marriage.

"Should I inform the parents?" asked Pawan.

"No. It will be dangerous for them. You come alone to Mumbai the day after and stay at the YMCA. On Saturday morning, you meet us directly at Bandra Court at 11:00 a.m. as the Panditji will complete the wedding ceremonies by 10:30 a.m. at the Shiva temple in Bandra, and then Kusum and I will come to Bandra court at 10:45 a.m. Our registration slot is at 11:00 a.m. Once you reach the court call me. I will be waiting for you," said Shankara.

Two days later, when Pawan boarded the train from Chandigarh to Mumbai, three men from Vijay's team who were tailing Pawan also boarded the same train. Upon arrival, they followed him to the YMCA, and once he checked in, they informed Vijay, who took a flight the next morning and arrived in Mumbai at 8:00 a.m.

On arrival, Vijay was driven to the YMCA, where his team was surveilling Pawan. At exactly 10:30 a.m., Pawan got into an auto and left for Bandra, followed by Vijay and his goons. When Pawan got off the auto outside Bandra Court, it was 10:55 a.m. He stopped at the base of the court steps and called Shankara. Shankara and

Kusum appeared on the first-floor balcony in a few minutes and waved to him. He waved back and started climbing the court steps. He had hardly taken two steps when he felt a sudden shooting pain in his back, followed by the sound of a shot. He tried to turn, but a second bullet hit him on his cheek and threw him sideways.

"Pawan!" screamed Shankara as he saw his best friend being hurled sideways. Hearing Shankara shout out his name, Vijay, who was standing with a smoking gun next to an Audi, looked up. Shankara and he locked their gaze for a second, and then Vijay fired at Shankara. Shankara and Kusum ducked behind the balcony wall.

"You thought you could fool me?" shouted Vijay as he ran up the steps to the first floor.

Shankara grabbed Kusum and made a run for it. As they zig-zagged through the dark corridors of the court, Vijay and his goons chased them, firing blindly. A couple of bullets hit a few passers-by and injured them, but Vijay couldn't care less. He just wanted Shankara dead. The couple ran to the far end of a corridor and took the stairs down, which led them to the parking lot where Shankara's bike was parked. Even as a volley of shots pounded all around them, they hopped onto the bike and zipped off.

For a few minutes, everything seemed okay, and Shankara began to think they had lost Vijay. Then, a black Audi suddenly shot out of an alley, its tires screeching on the concrete road. It was Vijay; he had found them.

As Vijay chased Shankara and Kusum through the streets of Mumbai, his men kept firing at them until they ran out of ammunition. At 'Linking Road', Shankara's bike collided with a car, and they fell. The bustling streets were filled with the roar of engines and the blaring of horns as cars and buses weaved through the heavy traffic. Amidst the chaos, Shankara found himself facing Vijay, who stood over him with a gun in his hand.

Vijay had a cold, determined look and a wry smile on his lips. Behind Vijay stood four of his men, their expressions equally menacing.

Without a second to lose, Shankara dived forward, rolling on the pavement and yanking Vijay's leg. The sudden movement threw Vijay off balance, and the gunshot rang out, but the bullet whizzed harmlessly past Shankara. Vijay's men sprang into action, rushing towards Shankara. The first one, a burly man with a shaved head, swung a crowbar. Shankara dodged, the crowbar smashing into the asphalt, sending sparks flying. Shankara countered with a powerful uppercut, sending the goon staggering backwards into the path of an oncoming car. The driver swerved, honking furiously as the goon stumbled to the side. Another goon, a wiry man with yellow eyes, lunged at Shankara with a knife. Shankara grabbed the man's wrist, twisting it until the knife clattered to the ground. He delivered a swift knee to the goon's stomach, followed by an elbow to the back of his head. The goon crumpled to the ground, dazed.

The remaining two goons tried to flank Shankara, but he was too quick. He spun around, delivering a roundhouse kick to one goon's chest, sending him crashing into a fruit cart. Apples and oranges scattered across the street as the vendor shouted in dismay. A tall, muscular man, the last goon, threw a punch, but Shankara blocked it and countered with a rapid series of punches to the man's torso. Each blow landed with precision, and the goon gasped for breath, collapsing to his knees.

In the meantime, Vijay, having regained his footing, aimed his gun again. This time, Shankara was ready. He grabbed a nearby trash can lid and flung it like a discus. The lid struck Vijay's wrist, knocking the gun from his hand. Vijay cursed and charged at Shankara, fists flying. The two engaged in fierce hand-to-hand combat, dodging and striking with a flurry of movements. Vijay managed to land a punch on Shankara's jaw, but Shankara quickly recovered, countering with a powerful kick to Vijay's ribs. Vijay staggered back, clutching his side, but his eyes burned with fury.

Traffic continued to flow around them, drivers shouting and honking, but Shankara remained focused. He ducked under another swing from Vijay, grabbing his arm and twisting it behind his back. With a swift motion, he tripped Vijay, sending him sprawling onto the pavement. Shankara stood over Vijay, breathing heavily. Vijay tried to rise, but Shankara placed a firm foot on his back, pinning him down. Filled with rage due to the loss of his best friend, Shankara looked at Vijay and said, "You killed an innocent man, Vijay; you don't deserve to live." With a roar, he kicked Vijay hard in his face. Vijay's head snapped back, enough to crack his spine but not enough to kill him. "Death would have been a relief for you. You need to live and suffer," growled Shankara.

The defeated goons groaned and struggled to get up, but they knew the fight was over. Their leader lay bleeding and unconscious, and the look on Shankara's face told them that he was in a killing mood. Shankara could hear the sirens wailing in the distance, signalling the approaching police. He released Vijay and turned to the gathering crowd, spotting many people making videos of him, Kusum, Vijay and goons.

Shankara helped Kusum stand up and said, "Let's go." They quickly made their way through the throng of onlookers, blending into the busy streets as the police arrived to apprehend Vijay and his goons. As they disappeared into the urban jungle, Shankara knew they had been exposed.

"Is the fight over?" asked Kusum as she hobbled along.

"The fight is over, but the war has just begun," said Shankara.

True to his predictions, the fight videos went viral within an hour. Every media channel was talking about it. The media announced that Vijay was in a coma at JJ Hospital in Mumbai.

Back home, Ali Khan sent Pawan's body to his home in Morni and said to Shankara, "You need to get out of the country. Dhillon is doing a concert in Tirana, Albania. Go there and take Kusum with you. I have spoken to Dhillon and made all the arrangements."

"When do we have to leave?" asked Shankara.

"Tonight," said Ali Khan.

"But the show is next week," replied Shankara.

"Take a few days before and after the show. Spend some time with each other, away from all these troubles and violence. I will inform your families that you are okay," said Ali Khan.

When Anna learnt about Vijay, he was distraught, but his sadness turned to rage when he visited Vijay at the JJ Hospital's ICU. The doctors informed him that Vijay had gone into a coma. "We tried everything," said the doctor.

Wanting to avenge his son, Anna decided to take matters into his own hands. He returned to Morni and went straight to Sukhdev's house. Sukhdev and Manpreet were having dinner when he entered their house. He looked at Sukhdev and said, "My son is lying in an ICU like a vegetable, and you are enjoying a peaceful dinner?" He kicked the table. The food, the plates, and everything else on the table flew.

While the rest of his men held Sukhdev down, he grabbed Manpreet and yanked her to his side. Then he looked at Sukhdev and said, "My son is in a coma and my daughter walks around like the living dead. He took away my dream, my mother's dream. He took away everything dear to me. Now, I will take away from you what is dear to you. I am taking Manpreet with me. Tell Shankara to come and get her."

As he dragged Manpreet into the car, Sukhdev screamed, "My Shankara will come, and then there will be a Tandav. When my Shankara opens his third eye, you all will be burnt to ashes. If he sees even one scratch on Manpreet's body, he will peel every bit of skin from yours. Your days are numbered, Anna."

"Tell your Shankara I am waiting to see his Tandav. Even I need some entertainment," replied Anna as he pushed Manpreet into his SUV and roared off.

Chapter 9

Shankara was enjoying peace and love with Kusum in Tirana when he got a call from Ali Khan. "Your father called. Anna has kidnapped your mother and wants you to come and get her," he said.

"Thank you for informing me, Chacha. Do you have Anna's number?" Shankara asked calmly.

"Yes. I took it from Sukhdev because I knew you would ask for it. Tread carefully, my son," said Ali Khan.

After taking Anna's number, Shankara called him. Anna was having breakfast with Gauri and his mother, Rukmini, when his phone started ringing. He did not recognise the foreign number but still answered the call. He pressed the speaker button and said, "Hello!"

"Get your army ready, Anna; I am coming for you. I sent your son into a coma, but you, I will send you into eternal sleep. I will chop the hand that touched my mother. I will slice the tongue that abused my father. And then I will rip your bloody heart and feed it to your dogs. Tell your mother, tell Rukmini Devi, Shankara is coming."

A chill went down Rukmini's spine. She looked at Anna and asked, "What have you done with Manpreet?"

"I have brought her here with me. This was the only way to get Shankara here," said Anna, continuing his breakfast.

"Oh my god, what have you done? Even Ravan did not win after abducting Sita ma, and you abducted Manpreet?" Rukmini asked.

"Neither am I Ravan nor Shankara, Ram," scoffed Anna.

"You are right. He is not Ram. He is Shankara. You will not be able to withstand his attack. He will turn you into dust. Listen to me. Vijay got what he deserved; return Manpreet with dignity and save yourself," said Rukmini.

Anna angrily pushed away his plate and shouted, "Are you my mother or Shankara's? I have told you before. I don't need your dumb advice. I will deal with my life. I am not interested in politics or reputation. All I want to see is Shankara's dead body lying at my feet. And I know how to get it done." He called out to his new bodyguard and said, "Tell the driver to get the car ready. We're headed to Uttam's house."

The moment Anna left, Gauri and Rukmini went searching for Manpreet. They found her locked in one of the rooms on the west side of Anna's palatial mansion. The room had one barred window and a tough-looking guard outside.

"Move aside, I want to meet Manpreet," said Rukmini.

"B-but Anna Bhai told me not to let anyone in," stammered the guard.

"Without me, there is no Anna Bhai. Open the bloody door, now," Rukmini barked.

The guard, shaken, quickly opened the door and let them in. The moment Rukmini saw Manpreet, she folded her hands, and said, "Shankara is coming to get you. If he does, there will be a blood bath. Anna has made a terrible mistake. I apologise on his behalf. Please, come with me. Gauri will take you home."

As Rukmini bowed to touch her feet, Manpreet held her and made her sit beside her. Then she looked at Rukmini and said, "No, Rukmini Deviji. Hanuman had also told Sita ma to come with him, but she refused and said she would return only with Ram. In that period of time, a wife waited for her husband to rescue her and take her back home with dignity. In this era, a mother awaits her son to do the same. I will not leave this place. Now, I will return only with Shankara." She hugged Rukmini and whispered, "I know you are trying to save your son. But tell me, what would you have done if you were in my place?"

With tears in her eyes, Rukmini said, "You are right. I would have done the same." She wiped her eyes, looked at Gauri and said, "Your father has gone to make an alliance with Uttam. I know Uttam very well. He will not give anything for free. He will ask for his pound of flesh, which will be you. He will ask Anna to give your hand in marriage for his wayward son Akhilesh, and your father, his mind filled with revenge, will accept it."

Shocked that her father would be willing to sacrifice her at the altar to serve his ego, Gauri cried out in distress. "I will commit suicide, but I will not marry Akhilesh," wailed Gauri. Manpreet got up from her seat, hugged Gauri tightly and said, "Go to my elder son, Kishan. He will help you."

"Why would he help me? My father is after his brother," asked Gauri.

Manpreet smiled at Gauri and said, "Because he has loved you since childhood. He transferred to Morni to propose, but you chose to marry Shankara. He loved you enough to let you go. And he loves you enough to get you back and help you. You will be safest with Kishan. Go to him."

Chapter 10

In Uttam Singh's house, Anna sat across the table and said to him, "We have been enemies all our lives and have achieved nothing. I will bow out of the MLA race and support your candidacy, but in return, I want you and your entire gang to help me destroy Shankara."

Uttam Singh looked at Anna. A wry smile played on his lips as his beady eyes assessed Anna. He sipped his tea a couple of times and then finally said, "I am happy you reached out to me in your darkest hour, brother, but alliances have no meaning in our society. Only relationships work, Anna. I am more interested in forming a permanent relationship with you and your family."

"What do you want?" asked Anna.

"You see, I am not interested in becoming the MLA. I was only doing it to spite you," Uttam moved closer to Anna and said softly, "What I am interested in is your daughter. I want Gauri's hand in marriage for my son, Akhilesh. If you agree, I will support you and make *you* the MLA. I am happy to be seen as the in-law of the MLA. Now that your dumb son is in a coma, Akhilesh will be your number two and, after your time, the number one."

Anna knew Akhilesh was worse than Vijay—a drug addict. Anna looked at the repulsive Akhilesh sitting alone in a corner and weighed his options. Seeing Anna's hesitation, Uttam said, "This marriage can end a generational dispute. It can end all the sufferings between our two families and consolidate our hold on Morni. Gauri will reign over Morni like a queen; I promise you that. And I will even build a hospital in her name."

Uttam waited patiently for a few seconds, then got up. "Do we have a deal? If not, you can fend for yourself."

As Uttam turned to leave, Anna held his hand and said, "Deal."

"Great," said Uttam, sitting down with a wide grin. He then called out to his bodyguard. A 6 feet 7 inch giant walked in and stood in front of them.

"This is Bulldozer, a Ukrainian mercenary who has killed over 25 Russian soldiers with his bare hands. The war destroyed Ukraine. and now there is nothing to eat in that country, so I brought him here. You don't need my army against Shankara. Bulldozer is enough for him," said Uttam Singh.

Back in Anna's house, a grateful Rukmini dispatched Gauri to Kishan's house with a note from Manpreet. Hopeful, Gauri left Rukmini with tears and a prayer that Kishan would accept her.

Kishan was filing an FIR against Anna at the Police Station when a constable approached him and said, "Gauri madam is waiting outside in her car."

Surprised, he walked out to see Gauri standing beside her white Nissan. The look on her face told Kishan something was wrong. He walked up to her, held her shoulders and asked her, "What's wrong?"

In response, Gauri embraced Kishan tightly and started sobbing. Embarrassed by her sudden outburst and realising that the entire police station was watching them, he told her to sit in the pillion seat and drove away from the station area. He drove to

Sukhdev's house and stopped outside. "Tell me. What happened?" he asked, still sitting in the car.

Gauri told him everything that had happened and handed him Manpreet's letter. Then she clung to him and said, "I never knew you loved me. I am so sorry."

Kishan read his mother's letter and said, "In such a situation, this place is unsafe. Let's go to my police quarters. It is well-guarded."

Chapter 11

When Anna returned from Uttam's, it was way past midnight. The following day, he woke up late and assumed Gauri had gone to her clinic as usual. When he did not see her at supper in the evening, he asked Rukmini, "Do you know where Gauri is?"

"No. I have stopped involving myself in this house. You deal with things from now on," said Rukmini, walking off to her room. Sitting inside, she could hear Anna huffing and puffing as he struggled to trace Gauri. Then she heard him talk to Uttam on the speakerphone, "Gauri is missing. I suspect Sukhdev's hand in this. He may have abducted her because I took Manpreet."

"You stay out of this for the moment. I am sending Akhilesh to Sukhi's." Uttam replied. Then he called Akhilesh who was in Chandigarh and said, "Take a small team to Sukhi's house and bring Gauri back."

"Sure. But not before I rip Sukhdev's heart out," said Akhilesh. Then he snorted some coke and said to his men, "Let's go."

Kishen sensed retaliation was inevitable. Without wasting a moment, he ordered Sukhdev to head to his police quarters a few kilometres away and stay with Gauri, far from the danger that was closing in. Then, he called upon his most trusted allies—the Rohtak team.

After a gruelling five-hour drive from Kunnar, the Rohtak team reached Morni at precisely 8:00 pm. They quickly refreshed themselves with a shower and a light meal, knowing the calm wouldn't last. As darkness enveloped the land, they took positions around the house, bracing for the storm.

The night was thick with tension. The sun had long sunk below the horizon, and a full moon hung high in the sky, casting a cold silver glow on Sukhdev's house. It stood defiantly at the edge of his mortgaged farmland, surrounded by an ominous wall of mangroves. The wind whispered through the trees, and the silence was heavy. They waited, knowing the assault was only a matter of time.

Everything was quiet in and around the house. At 8:30 p.m., the tranquillity of the night was suddenly shattered by the roar of engines as Akhilesh and his men arrived. Their vehicles kicked up dust as they screeched to a halt in front of the house. The air was thick with tension, and the smell of gasoline lingered. Inside the house, Kishan and the Rohtak cops were prepared. They had taken strategic positions, their eyes scanning the area with hawk-like precision. Kishan, who had dealt with encounters in Kunnar with the Rohtak cops, signalled to his men to stay alert. The Rohtak cops were known for their bravery and sharp shooting, and tonight, they would need every ounce of their skill as Akhilesh and his goons were armed to the teeth.

Akhilesh and his men cautiously approached the house, their guns ready. Known for his eccentricity and reputation for brutality, Akhilesh, barked orders to his men, his eyes fixed on the house. "Spread out! Make sure no one escapes! I want the father and son riddled with bullets but not a scratch on Gauri. Once the father and son are dead, I will escort her home," he said.

As the men fanned out, the first gunshot rang breaking the eerie silence. It came from a window on the second floor, where one of Kishan's men had spotted a man creeping towards the back entrance. The bullet went through his skull, and the man dropped to the ground dead.

And then, the gunfight erupted in full force.

Bullets flew in all directions, ricocheting off walls and shattering windows. Kishan, positioned behind an overturned table in the living room, took careful aim and fired. The bullet hit the man in the chest. The goon screamed in pain for a few minutes, crawled behind a parked car and died.

Two of Akhilesh's men managed to breach the front door, but the Rohtak cops were ready. They unleashed a hail of bullets, spraying the intruders with bullets. One goon died on the spot. The other, desperate, fired wildly, his shots pinging off the walls but missing their marks. The Rohtak cops returned fire with deadly accuracy, taking him down. As the Rohtak cops took down one goon after another, Kishan moved with calculated precision, signalling to a cop to cover him as he advanced. He spotted Akhilesh near the back of the house, trying to rally whatever was left of his goons. Kishan aimed and fired, the bullet went grazing Akhilesh's arm, causing him to yelp in pain and drop his gun.

Realising they were outgunned and outmatched, the remaining gangsters began to panic. One attempted to flee, but a Rohtak cop, perched on the roof, picked him off with a single shot. Another man, hiding behind a tree, tried to make a run for it but was quickly intercepted by Kishan, who tackled him to the ground and shot him point blank.

Akhilesh, clutching his wounded arm, stumbled back towards his vehicle, but Kishan was on him in an instant. He grabbed Akhilesh by the collar and threw him against the hood of the car, pressing his gun to Akhilesh's temple. "It's over. You're not going anywhere," he hissed.

Seeing their leader captured, the last two men made a dash for their car, but the Rohtak cops took them down one by one. Kishan heard the sound of sirens and knew the reinforcements were arriving. Within minutes, the flashing lights illuminated the scene of the fierce gunfight. The Morni police secured Akhilesh in handcuffs and read him his rights, as the Rohtak cops loaded the dead bodies into Akhilesh's SUV, drove it to Uttam's house and left it outside the main gate as a message from Kishen.

As the adrenaline began to fade and was replaced by a sense of accomplishment, Sukhdev's house, though battered and bullet-ridden, stood as a testament to the bravery and skill of Kishan and his Rohtak team. As Akhilesh was led away, Kishen surveyed the scene, ensuring all his men were accounted for. He nodded satisfactorily, knowing they had thwarted a dangerous criminal and his gang.

Later that night, as they sat in the living room and sipped their drinks, Kishan said, "This is not over. Uttam will come with a bigger force."

"Let them come. We are going nowhere," said the Rohtak cops.

Chapter 12

Bulldozer saw the SUV with the dead bodies at 5:00 a.m. when he stepped out of Uttam's mansion for his morning run and immediately informed his boss.

"Is Akhilesh there?" asked a worried Uttam.

"No." He was about to say something when a man came running and said, "I just heard that there was a deadly gunfight at Sukhdev's house, and Akhilesh Baba has been arrested and taken by the cops."

"Get the car ready; we are going to the police station," said Uttam.

Another man came running and said, "Boss, the station master at Morni Railway Station said Shankara and another man have arrived in Morni. They rented a Thar and drove off. The car rental reported they were going to Annaji's house."

It was 5 km from Morni Railway Station to Morni market and 300 yards from the market to Anna's house. The road ran straight to Anna's gate, with only one small crossroad in between. Uttam informed Anna about the situation. Anna spread his army in groups of six and placed them 100 yards from the market to the junction. Uttam sent 'Bulldozer', who stationed himself at the crossroads. Then, with 10 of his best men, he departed for the Police Station.

It was 8:00 a.m., and the harsh sun was already beating down on Morni Police Station. Tension was palpable as Uttam arrived with 10 of his most dangerous men. Their vehicles screeched to a halt in front of the station, and the gang emerged, heavily armed and ready for a showdown.

Inside the station, Kishen stood alongside the Rohtak cops and the local Morni police team. They had anticipated this attack and had taken strategic positions throughout the station and its grounds. The air was thick with the anticipation of the imminent confrontation.

"Release my son or face the consequences," shouted Uttam outside Morni Police Station.

"Come and get him," Kishan shouted back.

Uttam looked at his men and pointed at the Police Station. As he and his men approached the station, Kishen gave a silent nod to his team. The officers tightened their grips on their weapons, their eyes sharp and focused. The Rohtak cops were positioned at the windows and rooftop, while the Morni police, familiar with the terrain, took cover behind parked vehicles and hurriedly prepared barricades.

The first shot was fired by one of Uttam's men, shattering the window of the police station. It was the spark that ignited the fierce gunfight. The cops responded immediately, unleashing a hail of bullets that forced Uttam's men to scatter and take cover behind their vehicles.

Kishan, positioned at the front entrance, aimed carefully and fired, hitting a man inching closer to the building. The man dropped like a pole-axed steer, his gun skittering across the pavement. The Morni police, under Kishan's command, moved with practised precision, taking down two more men who tried to flank the station from the side.

On the rooftop, the Rohtak cops provided cover fire, picking off Uttam's men with deadly accuracy. One of them, a marksman named Raghav, spotted a man attempting to scale the side of the building. Raghav took a deep breath, steadied his aim, and fired, the bullet struck the climber squarely in the chest. The man lost his grip and fell to the ground, lifeless.

Seeing his men fall, Uttam roared in anger and began firing wildly at the station. Kishan, undeterred, signalled for his team to hold their ground. He stepped out from behind cover and returned fire, his shots forcing Uttam to duck behind a vehicle.

Two of Uttam's men managed to breach the station's perimeter but were met with fierce resistance from the Morni police. Inspector Verma, a veteran officer in the Rohtak team with a stern demeanour, took down one man with a well-placed shot to the leg, and his partner swiftly subdued the other with a powerful strike from his baton.

The gunfight raged on, the air filled with the loud sounds of gunfire and the shouts of officers and criminals alike. Uttam's numbers were dwindling, but he continued to fight with a ruthless determination. Hiding behind a car, he fired at Kishan, who dodged the bullets and advanced with unwavering resolve.

By the time Kishan reached the car, both he and Uttam were out of bullets forcing them to a fist fight with each other. The two grappled fiercely. Their weapons forgotten, they fought hand-to-hand. Kishan landed a solid punch on Uttam's jaw, but Uttam retaliated by delivering a knee to Kishan's ribs. They rolled across the ground, each struggling for the upper hand.

Meanwhile, outnumbered and outgunned, the remaining gangsters began to fall. The combined forces of the Rohtak cops and the Morni police overwhelmed them. One by one, the men were shot down, their weapons clattering to the ground as their lifeless bodies hit the dusty road outside the station.

His face set in a grim expression, Kishan finally managed to pin Uttam to the ground. He twisted Uttam's arm behind his back and pressed his knee into the criminal's spine. "It's over, Uttam," Kishan growled. "You're finished." As they stood up, Uttam slipped out of Kishan's grasp, grabbed a gun that was lying on the ground and aimed it at Kishan. But Kishan was too quick for him. He dived, picked up another weapon from the floor and fired while getting up. A trained double tap to the forehead flung Uttam six feet back. His body crashed against his SUV and slipped down lifelessly.

The sun continued to blaze in the aftermath of the battle. The Morni Police Station was bullet-ridden and battered, but inside, Kishan and his police officers were in a jubilant mood.

As the bodies of Uttam and his men were taken away in their vehicles, Kishan took a moment to survey the scene. He exchanged nods with his fellow officers, knowing they had faced a formidable enemy and emerged victorious.

Chapter 13

It was 9:05 a.m. when a black Thar screeched to a halt on the dusty street of Morni market. The two front doors opened as the dust settled, Shankara and Ali Khan stepped out. Both had Glocks in their hands with a Bowie knife tucked in their waistband.

Anna's men were surprised, as they did not expect Ali Khan to be with Shankara. The two looked at the long, straight road in front. The pockets along the three hundred yards were filled with Anna's men, each group of six lying in wait. At the far end, the imposing figure of the Ukrainian Hulk, Bulldozer, stood like an ominous sentinel, his bulging muscles glistening under the morning sunlight.

Ali Khan glanced at Shankara and nodded. "I'll handle Bulldozer," he said, his voice steady and resolute. Shankara returned the nod, gripping his Glock tightly.

A bloody fight was about to begin.

With synchronised precision, they moved forward, their steps silent and deliberate. The first group of men emerged from the alleyways, with guns raised. Shankara and Ali Khan wasted no time. Shankara's Glock barked twice, dropping two men before they could react. Ali Khan moved like a phantom, his knife flashing in the sunlight as he slit the throat of the third man, then pivoted to shoot the fourth in the chest.

The remaining two men lunged at them, but Shankara was ready. He blocked a punch with his forearm, then delivered a bone-crunching elbow to the man's face, sending him sprawling. Meanwhile Ali Khan, disarmed the last man with a swift kick to the wrist, then drove his knife into the man's side, twisting it to ensure he wouldn't get back up.

They pressed on, each step bringing them closer to Anna's house. Another group of six men emerged, but Shankara and Ali Khan were in perfect sync. They moved like dancers in a deadly ballet—their actions fluid and precise. Shankara shot a man in the kneecap, then spun and fired a headshot at another. Ali Khan used his knife to deflect an incoming blade, then followed up with a brutal series of punches that left his opponent crumpled on the ground.

As they advanced, the road grew slick with blood, the bodies of Anna's men littering their path. The fight intensified as more men poured out from hidden alleys and doorways. Shankara's Glock clicked empty, and he holstered it, drawing his knife.

The close-quarters combat became even more brutal. Shankara ducked under a wild swing, then drove his knife into a man's abdomen, pulling it out with a spray of crimson. Ali Khan faced off against two men at once, his movements a blur. He parried a knife thrust, then delivered a devastating kick to one man's knee, shattering it. The other man tried to shoot him, but Ali Khan knocked the gun aside and plunged his knife into the man's heart.

Finally, they reached the end of the road. Bulldozer cracked his knuckles and stepped forward, a cruel smile spreading across his face. "You're dead," he growled.

Ali Khan met his gaze with a steely determination. "Not today," he said as he stepped forward. The two titans clashed; their fight was a spectacle of raw power and skill. Bulldozer swung his massive fists, each blow capable of breaking bones, but Ali Khan was faster.

He dodged and weaved, landing precise strikes on Bulldozer's ribs and kidneys. The mercenary roared in fury, grabbing Ali Khan by the neck and lifting him off the ground.

Shankara, having dispatched the last of the gangsters, turned to help. He sprinted forward and leapt, driving his knife into Bulldozer's shoulder. The giant bellowed in pain, releasing Ali Khan, who dropped to the ground and rolled away. Together, Shankara and Ali Khan attacked Bulldozer with coordinated ferocity. Ali Khan struck low, aiming for the knees, while Shankara targeted the upper body. Bulldozer, overwhelmed, stumbled back, blood streaming from multiple wounds. With a final, desperate effort, Ali Khan delivered a crushing punch to Bulldozer's throat, collapsing his windpipe. Bulldozer fell to his knees, gasping for air, before toppling over, lifeless.

Breathing heavily, Shankara and Ali Khan stood over the fallen mercenary, their bodies covered in blood and sweat. They exchanged a weary glance. Ali Khan nodded to Shankara, who wiped his face with his hand and moved forward. Anna's house loomed ahead, a fortress waiting to be breached.

"Let's finish this," Shankara said, his voice unwavering. Ali Khan nodded, and together, they marched forward, ready to face whatever awaited them inside. When they entered Anna's compound, Shankara roared, "I am here. Face me like a Jat, you coward." As Shankara's voice echoed, Anna appeared on the terrace holding Manpreet. He had a rifle barrel to her throat. He looked at Shankara and said, "If you come any closer, I will kill your mother." Then he took another step forward and asked, "Where is Gauri?"

Before Shankara could reply, a white Nissan entered Anna's compound. The driver's door opened and Gauri stepped out. Kishan and Sukhdev got out from the rear doors. "I am here, father. Now let Manpreet Aunty go."

Anna gave a wry smile and let go of Manpreet. Then he pointed the rifle at Shankara and said, "You would have made a good son-in-law." Saying that, he aimed. He was about to pull the trigger. When a gunshot rang out. The bullet hit Anna's rifle and flung it away from him. Surprised, Anna turned to see Rukmini standing far away on his left, holding a gun. She looked at Manpreet and said, "Go to your son. I will deal with mine."

As Manpreet passed Rukmini, she whispered, "Thank you."

For a split second, Rukmini turned her gaze towards Manpreet. That was enough for Anna. He dived to the ground, rolled over and disappeared over a small wall.

While Sukhdev helped Manpreet into the white Nissan, Shankara ran after Anna.

As he passed Rukmini, he asked, "Where could he be?"

"Whenever he was scared, as a child, he would hide in the library," said Rukmini.

"Thank you," Shankara raced to the library. Gauri also followed him.

The dimly lit library of Anna's mansion was filled with an eerie silence, broken only by the soft sound of the wind brushing against the pages of books long forgotten. Shankara moved stealthily through the towering bookshelf, his eyes scanning the shadows for any sign of Anna. The scent of old paper and leather bindings mingled with the tension in the air.

Finally, he spotted Anna near the back of the library, standing before a large, antique desk. Shankara stepped forward, his movements deliberate and menacing.

"So, today, everything ends, Anna," Shankara said, his voice low and dangerous.

Anna sneered, his hand sliding into his jacket to retrieve a concealed weapon. "You think you can take me down, Shankara? I've survived worse than you." With a swift motion, Anna pulled out a dagger and lunged at Shankara. Shankara sidestepped, narrowly avoiding the blade, and countered with a powerful punch to Anna's jaw. The blow sent Anna staggering back against a bookshelf, books spilling onto the floor around him. Anna recovered quickly, his eyes burning with rage. He slashed wildly with the dagger, but Shankara was ready. He dodged each strike with fluid grace, his focus unwavering. Seizing an opening, Shankara grabbed Anna's wrist, twisting it until the dagger fell from his grasp. With a quick kick, he sent the weapon sliding across the floor.

Enraged, Anna swung a desperate punch at Shankara. Shankara caught Anna's fist mid-air, then delivered a bone-crunching knee to Anna's ribs. Anna gasped for breath, doubling over in pain, but Shankara was relentless. He grabbed Anna by the collar and threw him against the desk, the wood creaking under the impact. The Ray–Bans he always wore on his collar at the back flew and landed on a chair.

Anna grabbed a heavy book from the desk and swung it at Shankara's head. Shankara ducked, and the book smashed into a nearby lamp instead, shattering it. Using the distraction, Anna lunged forward, attempting to tackle Shankara to the ground. Shankara anticipated the move and used Anna's momentum against him. He twisted, sending Anna crashing into a bookshelf. The impact knocked several books loose, burying Anna under a pile of hardcovers. Shankara moved in quickly, delivering a series of precise, punishing blows to Anna's face and ribs, each strike landing with brutal efficiency.

Bloodied and battered Anna tried to fight back, but he was no match for Shankara's skill and determination. With a final, devastating uppercut, Shankara sent Anna sprawling to the floor, his body limp and defeated.

Breathing heavily, Shankara stood over Anna, with a bowie knife in his hand. With a loud roar he swung the blade up to bury it deep in Anna's heart. And then, he heard a familiar cough. He stopped midway and turned to see Gauri standing near the door with folded hands. Tears were streaming down her face. She shook her head, silently pleading with him to spare her father's life.

Shankara looked at her for a few seconds, then turned to Anna, "You are alive because of your daughter. The same daughter you were ready to sacrifice for your personal gain. If I ever hear you troubling anyone, I will be back." He kicked Anna in the ribs and walked out of the library. Behind him, Gauri ran to her father to help him.

Epilogue

Sukhdev and Shankara stood in front of a building. The board at the front read, 'Collector Coaching Institute'. Inside, there were several men, working out in the gym.

"What are you coaching?" asked Sukhdev.

"I am grooming bodyguards," said Shankara.

"Good. If not a collector, at least a Collector's Coaching Institute," he mocked looking at the sign board.

"This institute gives me more money than a collector's salary. And I have one more thing to prove my capability," said Shankara.

"What is that?" asked Sukhdev.

Shankara handed him Anna's Ray-Bans and a folder. "Both given by Anna," he said.

Sukhdev looked at the papers in the folder. It was the farm and house documents. With a big smile, he hugged Shankara and whispered, "I accept. You are my Shankara." Then he wore the glasses and asked, "Anna gave these to you or did you take them from him?"

"Does it matter?" asked Shankara.

"No," said Sukhdev and they burst out laughing.

Jugnu Joshi

Jugnu Joshi is the story of one man's fight for honour and justice in a world where the Police and the courts are infected with the 'My side bias' syndrome.

'My side bias' is the tendency to favour a biased belief and go on to confirm it through various forms of justifications.

In India, people often end up wrongly in prison because of this syndrome.

Wrongly accused and sentenced to fifteen years for a crime he didn't commit, 22-year-old Jugnu loses hope until a jail superintendent inspires him to fight for justice from behind bars. Dreaming of becoming a criminal lawyer, he challenges the corrupt system. Will he succeed? Can he reform the prison system?

Justice hangs in the balance.

Prologue

'Dasara Jail' was a high-security prison in the district of Kolhapur in Maharashtra. It was built on 139 acres of land and harboured 560 criminals. Blocks A1 & A2 were the transit blocks for petty criminals brought in for minor crimes. The accused were housed in the blocks till they were tried. Blocks B & C housed female inmates located a few hundred yards away from the men's cell and separated them by a fifteen-foot concrete wall. Blocks D, E, F & G housed male criminals with F & G specifically for those who had committed crimes that warranted extended sentences with or without a parole option. When Arjun Bangar, aka Jugnu, a youngster from the Wanjari caste in Maharashtra, was brought into Dasara Jail on rape charges, he was twenty-two years old. He was convicted for raping a seventeen-year-old, Vijaya Bhonsle, the stepdaughter of the Principal Medical Officer (PMO), Madhav Bhonsle.

The case gained prominence as it was a high-profile crime related to the famous Bhonsle family in Dasara. Everyone knew the Bhonsles, as the Patriarch Sudhesh Bhonsle was the wealthiest merchant in town. His eldest son, Raghav Bhonsle, was the District Magistrate of Kolhapur, and his second son, Madhav, was the PMO of Dasara Government Hospital.

The case of 'Jugnu Vs the State of Maharashtra' came to be commonly known as the 'Dasara rape case'. It was an open-and-shut case as there was enough material evidence against Jugnu, and Vijaya had identified Jugnu as the perpetrator.

Chapter 1

Jugnu and his biological parents, Santosh Bangar and Maya Palav, hailed initially from Ajara, eighty-six kilometres from the main Dasara Chowk. Jugnu lost his mother when he was three. Maya, a nurse at the local government hospital committed suicide by jumping into the Ajara Nadi (Ajara River). After Maya's demise, Jugnu was left under the care of Santosh, a peon in Dasara Government Hospital. Santosh loved his drinks. He went from a weekend drinker—who drank with his friends to enjoy and celebrate—to an alcoholic after Maya's death. He was a peon by day and a drunkard by night. He spent most of his time with a bar dancer, Shivani and ignored Arjun because he felt Arjun was a bad omen and was responsible for Maya's death.

Arjun's childhood was spent mainly with a loving, aged spinster neighbour, Kantha Joshi, who fed, bathed, and cared for him. Seeing his energy and positivity, she nicknamed him Jugnu. As a kid, Jugnu loved studying, so Kantha admitted him to the local government school, where he got a free education along with three meals daily.

After Kantha's death, Jugnu became alone again but somehow survived. At twelve, he started doing odd jobs for money required to keep his house running. After graduating from a local missionary-run college called Government Victoria College, Jugnu cleared the NET exam and became a junior lecturer in his alma mater, teaching math and science to junior college students. Jugnu's childhood love,

Vijaya Bhonsle, was one of his students. Though both were deeply in love, Jugnu was very conscientious and told Vijaya that he would marry her only after he was financially strong. Vijaya was a little insecure. Seeing his talents and ambitions, Vijaya feared she might lose him to someone else, so she decided to keep him close to her by making him her after-college tutor.

After Vijaya's biological father died in a road accident, her mother, Shanti, married Madhav. After marriage, Shanti and Vijaya moved into Madhav's palatial house. Madhav was a casanova and could not resist women. He continued having relationships with many women in Dasara, even after his marriage to Shanti. Often, the women in his life were happy to remain as his mistresses, but if anyone dared to blackmail him, he dealt with them severely through his childhood friend, the local SHO Vikram Gaitonde. Gaitonde was in charge of Dasara Police Station.

Gaitonde and Madhav's friendship was thicker than blood. If any of these women complained or tried to blackmail him, Gaitonde would threaten them with dire consequences.

Madhav disapproved of Vijaya's closeness to Jugnu, but Shanti felt nothing was wrong and allowed it. Jugnu and Vijaya loved the tuition arrangement as they could spend quality time with each other daily.

A year later, on a Friday, a day after Vijaya's seventeenth birthday, Madhav and Shanti were watching a movie at the New Cinema Hall when Gaitonde called him and said, "I have some bad news for you."

"What is it?" asked Madhav

"Jugnu has raped Vijaya. He was trying to escape, but we arrested him. He is in my custody at the local Police station."

Being the PMO, Madhav instructed Gaitonde to take Vijaya to his government hospital. At the hospital, Vijaya was medically examined by the shift doctor Dr Sebastian Joseph and declared raped. DNA testing of the body fluids and the skin cells under Vijaya's nails matched Jugnu's, and he was arrested. In court, Jugnu pleaded his innocence and told the Judge that he was a victim of circumstance and happened to be there at the wrong time.

"When I arrived, she was already raped. She was lying naked, bleeding, hooded and unconscious when I arrived. I tried to revive her, but when she regained consciousness, she attacked me, thinking I was the rapist."

The evidence was damning, so the Judge mocked Jugnu by saying, "And your body fluids got transported magically inside her, right?" As the entire court burst into laughter, Jugnu was sentenced to fifteen years in Dasara Jail. The case of 'Jugnu Vs the State of Maharashtra' came to be commonly known as the 'Dasara rape case, and it gained the attention of the whole nation.

To save her from the humiliation and shame that came along with being a rape survivor, Madhav and Shanti tried to get Vijaya married off. Unfortunately, the news had spread far and wide, and Vijaya's reputation preceded her, thus making it difficult for the parents to find an alliance for her.

Seeing their condition, Gaitonde stepped in and offered a solution. "My son Rupesh has always been in love with Vijaya. He never expressed it openly, as he knew about Jugnu and Vijaya's relationship. He spoke to me last night and said he is willing to marry Vijaya if she is okay. But before that, I need to know your views."

A grateful Madhav and Shanti agreed to the proposal and asked Rupesh to convince Vijaya. Rupesh chatted with Vijaya and told her about his wish to marry her. Vijay told Rupesh that after Jugnu's treatment of her, she was shaken and would take time to get over the trauma. Rupesh respected her needs and said he would wait till she got better. After a three-month wait followed by six months of courting, Vijaya gave in to Rupesh, and they married. When the news reached Jugnu, he was heartbroken. When Vijaya testified against him in court, he felt it could be because of a misunderstanding, but hearing the news of her marriage broke him.

Jugnu nursed his internal wounds in his solitary cell and silently blessed her, reconciling to the fact that now he had nothing to look forward to. Disappointed in life and God, he justified his condition to fate and decided to live his life in jail for the rest of his sentence.

The hopeless new chapter of Jugnu's life in Dasara jail began as he suffered through the daily struggle of prison. Initially, he was harassed in prison for raping a minor, but soon, the inmates forgot about him and left him alone. Left alone to himself, Jugnu became a loner but grabbed the attention of the Jail Superintendent, Ramesh Joshi. Jailer Joshi was a circle inspector living happily with his wife, Gomathi, and son, Suresh, in Kolhapur city.

Suresh had completed his B.Ed. and was planning to become a teacher in the local school, but unfortunately, one of his friends introduced him to a drug dealer who converted him into a drug addict. Once, he was caught stealing money from home for drugs, Gomathi tried to stop him. In the tussle between them in the apartment's balcony, Suresh lost his balance, went over the balcony and died. Based on witness reports of the neighbours, Gomathi was arrested and convicted of second-degree manslaughter without intention to kill and sentenced to five years in Dasara jail. Having lost his son and wife to the incident, Joshi requested the DGP Prisons for a transfer to Dasara jail as a warden so that he could be close to Gomathi. The empathetic DGP agreed, and Joshi joined Dasara as a Jailer.

Having gone through a tragic past and understanding what it felt to be imprisoned for being in the wrong place at the wrong time, Joshi empathised with Jugnu. Over the next few months, Joshi started observing Jugnu and concluded that he might be innocent after all. With Joshi and Gomathi having lost their son and Jugnu, his parents, the trio soon formed a strong bond over weekly lunches in prison. Jugnu became exceptionally close to Gomathi and looked up to her as his mother.

One day, Gomathi advised Jugnu to pursue law and become a criminal lawyer so that he could fight his case. Jugnu agreed to become a criminal lawyer but said he won't fight his case as he had nothing to look forward to.

"Even if I win the case, the society which has formed an opinion about me will never accept me back. In their eyes, I will always remain a criminal. At least here, I have respect, love and affection," said Jugnu.

"I will be released in a few years. What will happen to you then?" Gomathi asked.

"I am sure you will visit me regularly, and I will be happy with that," Jugnu replied.

"Okay. Then do me a favour; at least study and get your Law degree. We will discuss this again in a few years," said Gomathi.

Jugnu agreed, studied hard, and became a criminal lawyer. In the five years he spent studying law, he gathered a lot of knowledge and realised that accepting a wrongful conviction is also a crime. He discussed this with Joshi and Gomathi, and they convinced him to fight his case while in prison.

"All your study and hard work will go to waste if you don't prove your innocence. If you don't want to fight your case as Jugnu, let Jugnu fight Arjun's case and prove his innocence. Let this be an example of belief in life and the courts," said Joshi.

Inspired by Joshi's advice, Jugnu agreed, and together, they challenged the conviction and appealed to the High Court. With Joshi's influence and networking, the case got reopened.

"The case has been reopened. How do you prove you have been wrongly convicted?" asked Joshi.

"I cannot prove that as all the evidence is against me. My first step will be to prove the evidence is fabricated," said Jugnu.

"How do you do that?" asked the PI

"Since I know I never raped Vijaya, I know that the evidence was false and fabricated. I only have to prove that. On top of it, if Vijaya supports me, I could get the case suspended and apply for bail," said Jugnu.

"What do you need?" asked Joshi.

"I need your help," said Jugnu.

Chapter 2

As requested by Jugnu, Joshi began investigating the case again with the help of a Private Investigator (PI). With corruption a norm in most government institutions in India, the PI did not find it very difficult to gather copies of the medical report and Dr Sebastian's details.

"We have gone through every inch of the medical report. Everything seems to be in order. Even the signature on the report is from Dr Sebastian. What should we do now?" asked Joshi.

"Can you find out what really happened that night during the examination, when Vijaya was brought in?" asked Jugnu.

"How do I find that out?" asked the PI.

"Talk to the nurses. Find out if Dr Sebastian had falsified the reports or not," said Jugnu.

Three weeks later, the PI came to meet Jugnu. He had a big smile on his face. "What are you smiling about?" Joshi asked.

"You won't believe what I discovered," he said, placing a file on the table in Joshi's office.

"What is it?" asked Jugnu, irritated by the suspense.

"I bribed three nurses who were on duty that night. One of them was in charge of the shift, and one was in the examination room with the examiner," he said.

"That makes it only two. What about the third?" asked Jugnu.

"I am coming to that. But before that, I noticed you hadn't asked me who the examiner was," said the PI.

"Dr Sebastian, of course!" said Joshi.

"No,"

"Then who?" asked Jugnu.

"The examiner was none other than PMO Madhav himself," said the PI.

"Which is illegal. He is an affected party. A father examining his daughter is a '*conflict of interest.*' The report is not admissible," said Joshi with joy.

"The bigger question is, if he examined Vijaya, how did Dr Sebastian sign the report? He was the shift doctor. Why did he not examine her?" asked the PI.

There was a long silence, then Jugnu said softly, "Dr Sebastian was the shift doctor that night, but Madhav, his boss, instructed him to stand back. Madhav examined Vijaya, fabricated the report and asked Dr Sebastian to sign it."

"Why?" asked the PI

"Because Madhav knew he could not examine his daughter. He also knew that if he had told Dr Sebastian to fabricate it, there would be a witness to his crime who could blackmail him later. So, he found a better way out. He used his authority and power to replace Dr Sebastian. But he got Sebastian to sign it so that no one would suspect. The question is, how do we get Sebastian to confess?" asked Jugnu.

"Leave that to me," said Joshi.

The next day, three masked men entered Dr Sebastian's office, threatened him at gunpoint and got a written and video confession that he never examined Vijaya. Sebastian said the hospital was hectic that night due to the arrival of a large number of men who had consumed spurious hooch.

"The PMO told me he would step in and do the examination provided I sign it. I took it as help being offered. I never suspected anything," he pleaded on paper and in the video. Also, Joshi reached out Vijaya, who was now married and settled in Seattle with Rupesh, and told her everything that had happened.

"Jugnu has been wrongly convicted. The medical report was fabricated. At least now, tell us who examined you that night. It will save a life," pleaded Joshi.

A guilty Vijaya said, "Yes, I was examined by my father. He told me to keep quiet about it, or Jugnu would escape the conviction. I was so upset with Jugnu for betraying me that I agreed and kept quiet. I am sorry."

Jugnu approached the High Court with the new evidence and pleaded his case. Realising the damning proof being provided by Jugnu, Madhav appointed the best advocate in India, Senior Advocate Naresh Thambi. As Jugnu was taken to the High Court in the Police van in shackles and handcuffs, he asked Joshi, who was accompanying him, "Who did you send to get Sebastian's confession?"

"Three of my convicts who got released last week," said Joshi. Then he looked at Jugnu, and they burst out laughing.

After going through a three-month trial wherein Jugnu provided all evidence that the medical reports were tampered with: proof fabricated, medical examination conducted by a related party, and the shift doctor being an accomplice to the crime, the honourable judge of the high court listened to the arguments from both sides and finally gave his order. "The conviction is suspended, and Arjun Bangar can apply for bail."

A month later, Jugnu got bail and walked out of Dasara prison with Joshi, he found Gomathi, who was released a few months ago, waiting for him outside the prison. He hugged her tightly and asked softly, "Where do I go from here? I don't have a home. My father has sold the house we had and is now living with that bar dancer."

"Joshi and I have discussed this a long time ago. You are coming home with us as our son," said Gomathi.

Two months later, Joshi and Gomathi finished the adoption process, handed over the letter to Jugnu and said, "From this day, you are officially our son. Your new name is Jugnu Joshi."

Chapter 3

Out on bail, Jugnu cleared the bar exams and got approval to practise law. Gomathi opened a legal firm called *Jugnu Joshi Associates* and managed Jugnu's affairs while he fought the cases of all the under-trials in Dasara prison. Soon, the inmates started calling him 'Dasara Vakil'. While he never charged any fee from the petty criminals languishing in jail due to lack of representation, his reputation as a winning lawyer preceded him, and many hardened criminals started approaching him to fight their case… and Jugnu obliged by charging them hefty fees.

Soon, seeing his success rate, more influential prisoners started giving him their cases. He also won those and got paid more money. Every released inmate became his fan; some even joined him as employees. They all reported to Gomathi and helped Jugnu in his research, document gathering, show cause issuance, investigative work, filing FIRs, and other administrative work. In return, he used the fees to pay their salaries.

Though he had a flourishing business, tons of media attention and loving parents, Dasara Vakil was etched in the minds of the public not as a Criminal lawyer but as a lawyer for Criminals. Until one day, he had a visitor. The visitor's name was Dr Sumesh Keshavan, a renowned Malayalee cardiologist in Maharashtra and, more importantly, Joshi's close friend. Joshi introduced Jugnu to Keshavan and said, "I want you to fight Vinathi's case."

"Who is Vinathi?" asked Jugnu.

"Vinathi Keshavan is my sister. She is a budding actress who has done some TV Commercials in Kerala and Maharashtra. She recently completed the shoot for a web series in Mumbai," said Sumesh.

"What is her case?" asked Jugnu.

"She was raped three days ago," said Sumesh.

"Did you file an FIR?" asked Jugnu.

"We wanted to, but we can't," replied Sumesh.

Joshi explained the case to Jugnu. "The promoter of Elite Pictures, superstar Usman Ali raped her in his office during an audition session. Being a famous film producer and actor with a lot of clout in the Police and the government, no one wants to file an FIR, and no lawyer wants to take her case."

Jugnu thought for a while and said, "I am out on bail but accused of rape. If a so-called rapist takes a rape case, it is a recipe for disaster. It will fail before it even lifts off."

"If you help her get justice, the public perception about you of being a lawyer for criminals will change. The courts will also sit up and rethink their judgement. It will help you in your case whenever it comes up for hearing," said Joshi.

"You have a point." Jugnu looked at Sumesh and said, "Tell her to come and meet me tomorrow. Ask her to bring everything she has on the case."

When Sumesh told Vinathi that Jugnu would be fighting her case, she disapproved immediately. "If a rapist fights my case, we have lost the case even before it goes to court," she said.

"That is exactly what Jugnu said. He did not want to take up your case. But he is doing it now because of my request. Look, Vinathi, we have no choice. No one wants to touch your case. Our only option is Jugnu."

The next day, when Vinathi met Jugnu in his office, both were taken aback, as both felt the other was good-looking. "Tell me everything from the start," said Jugnu.

"Usman Ali is the MD of Elite Pictures. I am a budding actress, and I have done a few assignments, so when I heard that Elite Pictures was auditioning for a fresh face for their new movie, I applied. When I arrived for the audition, only Usman was in his office. He told me the scene required a home setting and took me to his residence, one floor above the office. Once in the living room, he gave me a script and told me to enact the scene. It was a scene where I was his wife, thrilled because he got promoted. I had to call out his name and run into his arms joyfully. The moment I ran into his arms, he grabbed me. I sensed something was wrong and tried to get out of his grasp, but he tightened his grip. I shouted at him to leave me. He refused, so I slapped him. Furious, he slapped me back hard a few times, dragged me into his bedroom, gagged me, tied my hands, and raped me."

"After raping me, he threatened me with dire consequences. He said if I opened my mouth, he would kill me and Sumesh. Then he threw me out of his house. After I left his office, I called Sumesh, who rushed me immediately to a private hospital. The Medical Officer on duty tested me, confirmed it was rape, and documented it in his medical report. We took the report and filed an FIR at the city police station, but the SHO refused to entertain us. He said if we escalated this further, he would slap a case against me for having sex with Usman with the sole purpose of blackmail and extortion. Additionally, by the time I got home, Rs 1 lakh was deposited in my account," concluded Vinathi.

"How did they know your bank account?" asked Jugnu.

"Production houses reimburse the audition expenses incurred by candidates. I had sent the bank details to Elite a day before," said Vinathi.

"Got it. So, if you escalate it, they will show the deposit as part of the extortion." Jugnu thought for a while and asked, "Do you have any way of confirming that the SHO refused to file out the FIR? Is there any witness?"

"No," said Vinathi.

Jugnu thanked Vinathi and let her go. "I will call you if I need you. You can leave your number with me if you trust me," said Jugnu.

Vinathi wrote down her number on a piece of paper and handed it to Jugnu; just before leaving, she turned at the door and said to Jugnu, "I am sorry for my initial rudeness. I trust you." Before Jugnu could respond, she left.

After spending an hour with Jugnu, Vinathi started feeling comfortable and slowly changed her opinion about him. Soon, they started spending a lot of time together discussing the case, how to plan it, and how to approach the problem. Working with him, Vinathi also learned much about the courts and various aspects of law.

With Jugnu's help, Vinathi filed a 'Zero FIR' at a local police station. Based on the FIR, Jugnu filed a case in the trial court. The judge gave them a month for preparation and said the trial would start 30 days later.

While Jugnu stayed professional and focused on the case, Vinathi slowly started getting drawn towards him. She found him sincere to his job. Soon, the attraction turned into love. As the case discussions and investigations proceeded, chemistry developed between the two, and they started dating.

The next day, Jugnu found out who the SHO was in the City Police Station in Kolhapur. It was Inspector Anil Bajaj, who was known to be loyal to Usman Ali.

Jugnu called SHO Anil Bajaj and said, "Good morning, sir; this is Advocate Jugnu Joshi. I represent rape survivor Ms Vinathi Keshavan, who came to you to file an FIR a few days ago, but you refused despite her having a medical report from a private hospital."

"I cannot file an FIR because some budding actress wants to blackmail a superstar," replied Bajaj.

"All right. Thank you, Mr Bajaj," said Jugnu and disconnected. He picked up his dictaphone to check whether the entire conversation had been recorded. Satisfied with the recording, he called Inspector Shakeel Ahmed, the Karveer Police Station in-charge. Shakeel knew Jugnu as he had helped him with a case a year ago.

"Need a favour, Shakeel," said Jugnu

"What is it?" asked Shakeel.

"Need to file a Zero FIR at your police station," he said.

An FIR can be filed at any police station, and the police must record information from a complainant. It does not matter in which area the crime happened. If any police station refuses to file an FIR, the complainant can file the FIR at a police station in a different location. The police will record the information and then transfer it to the police station nearest to the crime scene. This is called Zero FIR.

"Why?" asked Shakeel

"Inspector Bajaj is refusing to file one."

"Who is the affected party?"

"Ms Vinathi Keshavan."

"Oh! The Usman Ali issue."

"Yes."

"Listen, if I file this, the Deputy SP will blast me. You know this is a sensitive case," said Shakeel.

"I have never asked for a favour before. This is the first time," replied Jugnu.

"Okay. Ask Vinathi to come by to the police station tomorrow morning," said Shakeel and hung up.

The next day, Vinathi filed a Zero FIR, which was transferred to the city police station. When Anil Bajaj learned what had happened, he panicked and called Shakeel. "Why did you do this?" he asked.

"I had no choice. It is a rape case. The girl brought the press, and they had a copy of the medical report from the private hospital that was recorded three hours before you refused her an FIR. You better take action; otherwise, Jugnu Joshi will file a case against you, too," said Shakeel.

A worried Bajaj called the Deputy SP and told him what had happened. "We have to take action, sir," he said.

"You guys are misfits. Go to Usman and get him to the station for routine questioning. Then, record the conversation and send me the report. Let the report read that Usman was not in town at the time of the rape. Rest I will manage," said the Deputy SP.

Based on the FIR, Jugnu Joshi filed a case against Mr Usman Ali. In the meantime, the Deputy SP spoke with the District SSP, who talked to the IGP of the Kolhapur range. The IGP spoke with an MP, who spoke to Judge Remya Kirloskar, who was to preside over the case. The MP tried to throw his weight around, but Remya—known for her integrity, cold-shouldered him.

Chapter 4

Four weeks later, the case came up for hearing at the District Court. Jugnu arrived on a motorcycle with Vinathi behind him, while Usman's lawyer, the reputed Advocate Naresh Thambi, arrived in a Honda Accord. Since it was a high-profile case, the media was there in full force.

The Judge arrived at 10:00 a.m., and the hearing began at 10:15 a.m. Jugnu Joshi opened the argument, "Good morning, your honour; we are here to establish that Mr Usman Ali committed the act of rape on my client, Vinathi Keshavan."

Judge Remya looked at Thambi and said, "Senior Advocate, Mr Thambi, would you please make your opening remarks?"

"Thank you, your honour. The so-called rape victim, Vinathi Keshavan, is a blackmailer and has already extorted Rs 1 lakh from my client Usman Ali. When Usman refused more, she said he raped her. We will establish that she is a fraud and an extortionist."

"You are a senior lawyer, Mr Thambi. You are well aware that it is against the law to use the word 'victim' in the case of rape. Please use the word 'survivor' henceforth," said Judge Remya. Then she looked at Jugnu and asked him to proceed.

"Your honour, the Defence would like to call upon the accused, Mr Usman Ali," said Jugnu. When Usman Ali took the stand, Jugnu asked the routine inaugural questions about name, profession, and other things, asking, "Do you know Ms Vinathi Keshavan?"

"Yes. She came for an audition a few days ago," replied Usman.

After a long silence, Jugnu suddenly asked, "Did you rape Vinathi Keshavan, Mr Ali?"

Usman was stunned by the direct question and took a few minutes to recover before saying, "No. I did not."

Jugnu walked up to Usman and said softly, "I have the clothes you wore the day you raped her, Usman. I got it tested as well. Your shirt has Vinathi's saliva and sweat stains and hair from the survivor's private parts. I will ask you again, did you rape Vinathi?"

SHO Bajaj looked at the Deputy SP sitting in court and rolled his eyes. The Deputy SP was looking worried, and his face was pale.

Usman looked at Jugnu confidently, "I don't know how all that got there. I never touched her. When I told her she was not the type of actress we were looking for, she demanded money from me. I refused, and she stormed out, saying she would fix me."

"Mr Usman Ali. You will only answer the questions that have been asked. Anything more you say will be held against you. Jugnu, please continue," said Judge Remya.

"No. I did not rape her," Usman Ali replied with a wry smile on his face.

Since Thambi had no questions for Usman, Jugnu called SHO Anil Bajaj to the stand. "Mr Bajaj, did Vinathi come to file an FIR at your police station?"

"Yes. She did. I told her I cannot file the FIR without an investigation, which is underway as we speak," said Bajaj.

"And did you conduct an investigation, sir?" asked Jugnu.

"Yes, I did both on Usman and her. I found no proof of rape

in his house, but I surely did notice a 1 lakh debit in her account minutes after the so-called rape."

"So, you concluded it was a blackmail extortion debit? Why did you not think it could be a token advance for her role in the new movie they were auditioning for?" asked Jugnu. As Bajaj stuttered for a reply, Jugnu added, "It was all planned. When things went out of hand, he paid, tried to make it look like an extortion payment, and you are now seconding it."

He dismissed him without giving Bajaj a chance to retort and called Constable Suleiman to the stand. "Constable Suleiman, how many months left until your retirement?"

"Three months, sir," replied Constable Suleiman.

"You have spent over four decades in the Police force and have an impeccable record. No wrongdoings and no adverse reports. A simple question. Is there any investigation going on?"

"No, sir. I was told to call Usman over and do a routine questioning and then file a report as given to me by my senior."

"And what does the report say?"

"That Usman was not in town during the time."

"Did you investigate if he was or wasn't there at his residence during the rape?"

"No sir. I was told not to."

"Your honour, please note that Constable Suleiman has said on oath that neither did he investigate Usman; nor is there any investigation underway as Mr Bajaj would want us to believe. To top it, Constable Suleiman was asked to fabricate a report stating the accused was out of town." Jugnu placed a document in front of the judge and said, "My lord, the call records of the said date show Usman had multiple conversations with Bajaj, and as per the tower report, Usman was making the calls from his residence. He was in town."

"I agree with all this, and there is sufficient proof to take action against the Police force, but it still does not prove that Usman Ali raped Vinathi," said Judge Remya. Precisely at that moment, Gomathi walked in with two USB sticks.

"Your Honour, I agree, but this new evidence will prove the rape." Jugnu handed one stick to the judge and the other to Thambi and said, "I apologise, I could not share this before as I just received it. I request you to view it."

Judge Remya viewed the video on the stick and said to Thambi, "This video proves he raped her. This is a live recording of the incident."

"This is inadmissible, my lord. I have not had time to review it," said Thambi, realising he had lost the case already.

"I will give you three hours to review and come back. The court will resume at 3:00 p.m.," Judge Remya said, hitting the gavel on the wooden top and leaving.

As soon as she left, Thambi walked over to Jugnu and said, "Are you ready for an out-of-court settlement? My client is willing to pay the price the survivor asks."

"I will mention my demands at 3 p.m.," said Jugnu.

When the court re-convened, Jugnu said, "The learned Thambi sir has offered a generous out-of-court settlement, but unfortunately, this case is not just about rape but about a larger nexus. Hence, I cannot accept the offer."

"What larger nexus?" asked Judge Remya.

"This is not just a case of rape. It is a case of a full-fledged porn business Usman Ali is running. The quality of the recording, the angle of the recording and the lighting clearly shows this rape was pre-planned," said Jugnu.

"This is preposterous, my lord. My friend Jugnu has nothing to prove his allegations," Thambi shouted.

Jugnu smiled at Thambi and said, "I have all the proof. My PI is a tech wizard. He has traced a member-only porn site that specialises in rape videos. This is an exclusive website accessible to only 50 high-level, high-paying loyal subscribers. Each subscription has an annual charge of 1 crore rupees in cash. Usman gets 50 crore in cash every year, which he uses to produce his films. The black money from the porn business is laundered through his film production company." Jugnu handed Judge Remya a list and a copy to Thambi and said, "Those are the 50 subscribers, my lord. You may be familiar with many of the names in the list as some belong to your colleagues and some to the Police force. This is why no policeman or lawyer wanted to proceed with this case."

"You have anything to ask, say or comment, Mr Thambi?" asked Judge Remya.

Thambi, who was reading the list, looked shocked as he found the names of many senior bureaucrats, lawyers, judges, and Police officials on it. He looked at Judge Remya and said, "I have nothing to say."

Judge Remya passed the order two weeks later, on 8th January. Usman Ali was sentenced to fifteen years in prison. A new investigation was ordered on the porn case, and the names on the list were sent subpoenas asking them to present themselves in court to justify their subscriptions. The entire nation's media was focused on Jugnu. As they walked out of court, a reporter asked, "How sure were you that you will win?"

"Today is the 8th day of the new year. Number 8 depicts infinity, which is Mahadev's number. When the lord himself is with us, why doubt?" replied Jugnu.

The morning headlines on 9th January read, "Rapist wins a rape case."

Jugnu was very upset that the world still called him a rapist and restless with the excessive delays in his case hearing, "Unless my case comes for trial, I will never be able to prove my innocence and remove this '*rapist*' stigma attached to my name."

Gomathi was happy that Jugnu was desperate to fight his case. She approached Joshi and told him, "He wants to fight his case, finally. Please help him." Joshi pulled some strings in the judiciary through an MP he knew and announced the case hearing dates after a month's struggle. The first hearing date was given as March 7th. However, the caveat was that the case hearing must be completed within seven days as it was just a re-hearing of the existing facts presented during the earlier conviction. The court said if there is merit in a complete renewed investigation, then it would be decided later.

Once the dates were announced, Jugnu left everything and focused only on his case. As he investigated further, he traversed from one shock to another. Jugnu used every single resource he had to collate all the evidence. Vinathi stood by him like a rock and motivated him whenever he got stuck in his investigation. With Joshi, the PI and Khaleel helping him in his investigations, Jugnu was well prepared when the dawn of the new hearing arrived.

Chapter 5

It was the 7th of March, at 10:00 a.m., and the courtroom of High Court Judge PK Mahmood was jam-packed. Jugnu was in court early, as he wanted to arrange the documents to smooth the flow. Outside, the reporters announced to their respective channels, "Hearing on the *Arjun Bangar Vs the state of Maharashtra* case has begun."

Senior Advocate Thambi arrived at 9:30 a.m., and Judge PK Mahmood struck his gavel at 10:00 a.m. Immediately, Thambi got up and said, "My lord, let me present the facts to this court. Whilst Vijaya Madhav was expecting a happy married life with Arjun Bangar, he was just lusting for her. He had no intentions of marriage."

"That fateful evening at her house, when she resisted his advances, he, in a fit of rage, raped Vijaya. Unable to take the shock and the pain, Vijaya screamed. Arjun panicked and tried to escape, but SHO Vikram Gaitonde, who was passing by, heard her screams and ran into the house. Inside the house, Arjun was seen holding a knife in his bloodied hand while Vijaya was screaming for help."

"The FSL tests proved beyond doubt that Jugnu's skin deposits and blood traces were found in Vijaya's nails. This happened when Vijaya tried to fight him off. His body fluids were found in her private parts, proving he entered her. Also, the DNA report shows that Vijaya's hair and sweat were found on Jugnu's shirt. All the reports have been submitted to your lordship for perusal. Your

Honour, this is an open-and-shut case. My friend Jugnu Joshi is wasting the court's time."

Judge Mahmood, who had already gone through all the evidence, documents and reports, said, "I will decide whether the counsel is wasting the court's time or not, Mr Thambi." Then he looked at Jugnu and said, "Mr Joshi, would you like to counter the evidence, please?"

Jugnu stood up and said, "Yes, your Honour. Thambi sir is a learned advocate and much more senior than me. He has more wisdom and knowledge than me, but sadly, instead of using them, he is being cunning, which is the lowest form of wisdom, to justify the fabricated evidence used to misguide the court."

"I object, your Honour," Thambi said.

"To what?" asked Judge Mahmood.

"Jugnu is getting personal with me and judging my capabilities," said Thambi.

"Mr Joshi, kindly refrain from making personal remarks. Please continue," said Judge Mahmood.

Jugnu apologised to Thambi and Judge Mahmood and continued, "Your Honour, with your permission, I would like to draw the Honourable Court's attention to the DNA report. The report states that the skin deposits and blood traces found in Vijaya's nails belong to Arjun. That fact is correct. When the survivor Ms Vijaya regained consciousness, she saw Arjun in front of her, holding a knife in bloodied hands and assumed he had raped her. As a natural reaction, she attacked him and scratched him. The blood and skin tissue in her nails are because of that. It does not prove that he raped her. But from day one, the prosecution insisted that Arjun raped Vijaya."

Thambi laughed loudly.

"Anything funny, Mr Thambi? Can you share the joke with the court?" asked Judge Mahmood.

Thambi apologised and asked, "What about Dr Sebastian's vaginal swab report? Did Arjun's body fluids appear miraculously?"

"Mr Thambi, please address whatever you say to the court. Do not question Mr Joshi directly." Then he looked at Jugnu and asked, "What report is Mr Thambi talking about?"

Jugnu got up and said to the judge, "Your Honour, Mr Thambi is talking about the medical report submitted by Dr Sebastian Joseph. I have already proved that Dr Sebastian is not the author of that medical report; it was prepared by the PMO, an interested party in the case. The report was termed inadmissible in court during Arjun's bail hearing."

Judge Mahmood looked at Thambi and asked, "Is it true?"

Thambi nodded his head. "Then why are you discussing the report again?" asked Thambi. "This is called wasting court's time," the Judge added.

There was pandemonium in the courtroom, with people shouting and media personnel speaking. Judge Mahmood banged his gavel and said, "Order, order. The court will record again that Dr Sebastian Joseph did not examine the survivor, and the submitted medical report is null and void." Then he looked at Jugnu and Thambi and asked, "Are there any more debates or re-presentation of facts and evidence to counter anything discussed in the original arguments?"

"No sir," said both.

"In that case, I will give my judgment tomorrow." Judge Mahmood rose and left.

After a tense night, the court resumed the next day; the gavel in Judge Mahmood's courtroom hit the wooden block at 10:00 a.m. sharp. He looked at the media first, held up the newspaper of the day, where the headlines read, 'Dasara Vakil blows a hole in Thambi,' and asked, "What happened to journalistic decency?" He shook his head in disgust and addressed the court. "It has been proved beyond doubt by Mr Joshi that the evidence was fabricated by an interested party illegally to frame Arjun Bangar as Vijaya Madhav's rapist. At the time, the prosecution and the court relied on this fabricated evidence and convicted an innocent man. The court apologises to Arjun Bangar for its wrongdoing and declares Arjun Bangar innocent. It directs PMO Madhav to give a compensation of 5 crores to Arjun Bangar; 1 crore for each year of suffering in jail. The court also directs that the Vijaya Vs State of Maharashtra case be retried in the high court to find the real criminal behind this heinous act."

"Arjun Bangar is to be released from Dasara jail immediately," said Judge Mahmood as he banged his gavel again and stood up.

The newspaper headlines the following day read, *"Jugnu Joshi Strikes again."*

Chapter 6

It had been exactly 24 hours since Jugnu's release from prison. Since it was Sunday, Gomati had made an elaborate breakfast. As Jugnu, Joshi, and Gomati sat around the table, Joshi asked Jugnu, "So, what is your opinion on Vinathi, son?"

"She is nice," said Jugnu, knowing where the conversation was heading.

"Hmm… in that case, your mother and I have decided to get the two of you married. We spoke to Dr Keshavan, and he has accepted the proposal."

"What about Vinathi?" asked Jugnu.

"You need to ask her yourself," said Gomati.

"Sure. I will talk to her today. We are going to find a proper office in a commercial building. I can't operate from our home for the rest of my life," said Jugnu.

"Good. Then, while you are at it, look for an apartment as well. You can't keep living with us all the time," said Joshi. All three looked at each other and burst into laughter.

Jugnu and Vinathi left home at 9:30 a.m. to find an office. They had shortlisted a few places earlier and planned to spend the whole day visiting them one by one. Jugnu and Vinathi went all over the Kolhapur City but did not like anything. Their last stop was at an address exactly opposite Dasara jail. When they reached the address, they saw a red and yellow house. They rang the bell, and an old lady called Sita Tai answered the door. "We are here to see the office space," said Jugnu.

"This is the space," she said, taking them inside her cute two-bedroom house.

Though they were looking for an office space, they started loving it as they walked around the house. After the tour, Jugnu asked Vinathi softly, "Instead of looking for an office and house separately, why not buy this house and make one room the office?"

"I was thinking the same. Cost wise also, it will be better," said Vinathi.

"Are you willing to sell this Sita Tai?" asked Jugnu.

"If the price is right, I will consider it. I am also planning to return to my village and settle down," said Sita Tai.

One hour later, Jugnu finalised the price with Sita Tai and paid her an advance to close the deal. As they drove back, Jugnu realized that fate had got him in and out of Dasara Jail and finally brought him back next to it. He looked at Vinathi and saw her smiling.

"A penny for your thoughts," Jugnu said.

"You seem to have some previous connection with this jail," she replied.

Three weeks later, Jugnu and Vinathi got married. An emotional Sumesh held Jugnu's hands and said, "At one time, this society had rejected her. You gave her hope, then wings, and now a life. I am eternally indebted to you." Then he looked at all the released prison inmates who had come for the wedding and said softly, "This looks more like a mafia wedding."

A month later, the newlywed couple moved into their new home, *'Dasara Nivas,'* and converted one of the bedrooms into their office. They did not have to do a lot of preparation because all the families of the Dasara inmates were there to help. The arrival of goons and thugs to the office initially petrified Vinathi, but soon, she got used to them and dealt with them like regular clients. The money was good, and they even considered having a child. That is when Jugnu got a call from Joshi.

"Yes, Dad?" he said.

"I don't know if you will ever be able to forgive me, but I have kept something from you. We need to meet and speak. Come to my office. We will chat there," said Joshi softly.

Since Jugnu had taken the call on speakerphone, even Vinathi heard the conversation. "What could it be?" she asked Jugnu. Then she added, "He sounded serious, though. Better meet him quickly."

When the father and son met in Joshi's office in Dasara Jail an hour later, Joshi seemed worried.

"Blurt it out, Dad," said Jugnu.

Joshi nodded and said, "A few weeks ago, while you were busy with your case, I got a call from the lawyer in Mumbai. He represented a lady called Sudha Chandavarkar, who wanted to meet me urgently. She said she had something to discuss regarding you, so I went to meet her. We did not speak for long as she was on her deathbed, but I realised that she knew everything about you and us and wanted to reveal a secret before she died."

"What secret?" asked Jugnu.

"That she is your mother." Looking at the shocked expression on Jugnu's face, Joshi held his hands tightly and said, "I met Maya Pallav, your biological mother. She is alive but dying. I told Gomathi but not you, we felt you would be distracted. After winning the case, we thought we would tell you, but then we wanted you to settle down first and then tell you. I am incredibly sorry, Jugnu; please forgive us for being selfish."

Jugnu was silent for a bit as he controlled his emotions. Then he hugged his dad tightly and asked, "How is she?"

"Frail. She is in her final stages of Cancer. Chemotherapy has taken away her hair and sucked her from the inside. I wanted to take her picture, but she told me not to. She handed me a diary and made me promise to give it to you and you only." Joshi handed him a diary and said, "She told me to tell you that everything you ever wanted to know about your past is in here."

"Can I see her?" Jugnu asked.

"She told me not to bring you to her, but I think you should meet her," said Joshi.

Back home, Jugnu told Vinathi everything. Later in the night, he read the entire diary. There was an envelope taped to the last page, which had a simple one-page will. It had all the essential details like her personal information: The testator's name, father's name, home address, date of birth, and the declaration of date. Below that was a simple paragraph that read, *'I, Maya Pallav, a resident in the City of Mumbai, State of Maharashtra in India, being of sound mind, not acting under duress or undue influence, and fully understanding the nature and extent of all my property and this disposition thereof, hereby make, publish, and declare this document to be my Last Will and Testament ("Will"), and hereby absolutely revoke any and all other wills and amendments previously made by me. I, Maya Pallav, devise and bequeath everything I possess to my only son, Arjun Bangar, aka Jugnu Joshi.'* It was signed 'Maya Pallav' and notarized and stamped by her lawyer, making it a legal document.

Chapter 7

The next day, Joshi, Vinathi, Gomati and Jugnu flew to Mumbai to meet Maya. The lawyer received them at the airport and took them to an apartment on Nepean Sea Road. When Jugnu walked into the dimly lit room; he could smell her. With tears rolling down his eyes, he sat next to the frail lady with wrinkled skin and held her hand.

"How are you mother?" he asked her.

"I am happy now," she said, smiling at him. She caressed his face with her frail hands and whispered, "I am sorry. Please forgive me."

"Please don't be sorry…" Jugnu's voice trailed away as he realised that Maya had died in his arms.

After completing his mother's last rites, Jugnu and his family returned home to Dasara. The fact that he had become a millionaire did not even cross his mind because, after reading the diary, he was only obsessed with finding the criminal who had raped Vijaya and getting her justice.

A month passed since Jugnu discovered that his mother had lived up to 75 and died of cancer, leaving everything she owned to him. Jugnu and Vinathi, along with Joshi and the PI, used the month to conduct a thorough investigation of the case and collected every piece of evidence, witness statement and report necessary to fight the case. Once they had everything they needed, Jugnu called Vijaya and told her and Rupesh what he planned to do. Having realised the trauma and suffering Jugnu had gone through due to Vijaya's testimony in her case, the guilty couple agreed and officially hired Jugnu. Effective the 22nd of August, Jugnu Joshi was Vijaya Gaitonde's official lawyer.

Armed with the papers, he appealed to the high court for a retrial of Vijaya versus the State of Maharashtra. Then, he sent notices to Madhav Bhonsle, Raghav Bhonsle, and Vikram Gaitonde to appear as witnesses for examination. As expected, senior advocate Naresh Thambi represented the Bhonsles and Gaitonde.

With only three more months left to retire, the High Court appointed Justice PK Mahmood again to preside over the case. The hearing was scheduled for August 30th.

Chapter 8

It was August 30th, and the courtroom was packed with people and media. One could feel the room's excitement as everyone discussed the case. At sharp 10:00 a.m., Judge Mahmood's gavel hit the wooden block on his table. The loud sound quieted everybody.

Judge Mahmood looked at Thambi and Jugnu and said, "Since we are here today to start the process that will lead us to the real criminal behind Vijaya Bhonsle's rape, I am presuming both sides are on the same page."

Thambi stood up and said, "Your honour, during the first trial of this case, the honourable judge of the district court had accepted the evidence and declared Arjun Bangar the perpetrator of the crime. We request the honourable court not to entertain this re-trial, reverse the previous order, and put Arjun Bangar behind bars again."

Judge Mahmood glared at Thambi and said, "I know you are much wealthier than me, and the arrogance stems from that. But let me assure you that my years as a judge have made me much wealthier here," Judge Mahmood tapped his head and smiled sarcastically.

Then his face became serious. "Arjun Bangar was acquitted due to insufficient evidence of the crime. So, this case has no bearing on that. I will repeat it. We are here to find the real culprit in the Vijaya versus the state of Maharashtra case. Unless you have enough evidence to disprove Arjun's innocence, you better do an excellent job defending your clients, Mr Thambi."

Thambi glared back at the judge and said, "We will do just that, your honour."

Judge Mahmood shook his head in disgust, looked at Jugnu and said, "You may begin now."

Jugnu looked at Judge, bowed and said, "Let me begin by making a disclosure. Santosh Bangar is not Arjun Bangar's biological father."

For a few seconds, the court went silent as everyone was digesting this explosive statement. Then it erupted. The media ran in and out of the courtroom, trying to provide the scoop to their channel.

"Order, order," shouted Judge Mahmood, repeatedly striking his gavel on the wooden block until the room became quiet. "If anyone makes a stir in my courtroom, I will have him or her thrown out. It does not matter if you're from the media." Then he looked at Jugnu and asked him to continue.

Before Jugnu could continue, Thambi stood up. "Objection," he said.

Judge Mahmood looked at Thambi and asked, "To what? His name?"

Thambi said, "The Defence suspects this caveat may have some bearing on the case and hence demands proof that Santosh Bangar is not Arjun's biological father."

Judge Mahmood looked at Jugnu and said, "That is a fair request. Does this information have any relevance to this case? And if so, please give us proof of statement."

Jugnu handed a report to Judge Mahmood and said, "This is the DNA report of Santosh and Arjun. I got Santosh Bangar's DNA from the district hospital after getting his permission, your honour.

If you look at the report, it clearly says the DNA does not match."

"Santosh gave you permission to do a DNA test on him?" asked Thambi.

"No. My assistant Vinathi spoke to him and got his written permission." Jugnu handed over another paper with Santosh's signature on it. A smile came on Judge Mahmood's face when he noticed that the paper was a standard hospital blood test form with one additional column called 'DNA test'. At that moment, he realised he was dealing with a cunning lawyer.

"Then who is Jugnu's father?" asked Thambi.

"Arjun's biological father is Madhav Bhonsle," said Jugnu.

The courtroom erupted again despite Judge Mahmood banging the gavel. By now, all media channels across the country were covering Vijaya's case as Jugnu gave them one breaking news after the other.

"This is absolute rubbish," shouted Thambi.

Jugnu submitted the same blood test form, which had Madhav's signature on it. "Your Honour, the report confirms the match, and the form has been signed by Madhav Bhonsle."

Thambi looked at Madhav, who was sitting next to him and Raghav, and asked, "Why did you sign the form?"

"I did not know. This woman came home and made all of us sign individual forms saying this is a blood test for COVID," said Madhav.

Judge Mahmood nodded after looking at the report and asked Jugnu to continue.

Jugnu stood up and addressed the judge. "Your Honour, every act of crime has a motive, and there was a motive behind raping Vijaya Bhonsle as well. The motive was revenge. The case is complicated, and so is the act of revenge."

"Don't be so dramatic and come to the point," said Thambi.

Jugnu ignored Thambi and continued, "The perpetrator who raped Vijaya was taking revenge on Madhav, and the perpetrator who changed the course of the investigation was taking revenge on Arjun. Both criminals used the opportunity at hand to take their revenge."

"Could you care to elaborate Mr Joshi?" asked Judge Mahmood.

"Yes, Your Honour. But for that, I would like Madhav on the stand, please," said Jugnu.

"The court does not have that much time," said Thambi.

"Let me decide that. Permission granted," said Judge Mahmood.

The bailiff announced Madhav's name. Madhav walked up, took the stand, then the oath and then sat inside the witness box.

"Could you please tell the court who you are?" asked Jugnu

"I am Principal Medical Officer Madhav Bhonsle," said Madhav.

"Would you agree if I say you have a powerful motive to get your bastard son convicted?" asked Jugnu.

"No. I have nothing to gain by putting Arjun in Jail," said Madhav.

"PMO Madhav Bhonsle's bastard son getting married to his stepdaughter would have been too much to take. Is it not enough reason for framing Arjun and getting him out of the way?"

"Objection, badgering the witness," said Thambi.

"Overruled, continue Mr Joshi," said Judge Mahmood.

"I did not know that Arjun was my son," said Madhav.

"That is a lie, and I will prove it," said Jugnu. "I call upon Santosh Bangar to take the stand, please."

"Objection. Santosh is irrelevant to the case," said Thambi.

"He is extremely relevant and plays a crucial role in the case your honour," said Jugnu.

"Overruled. Please continue, Mr Joshi," said Judge Mahmood.

The bailiff called out Santosh Bangar, who walked in, took the stand, and took the oath. Once seated, Jugnu approached him. "Please state your name and occupation."

"My name is Santosh Bangar. I am a peon in the Government Hospital."

"How do you know PMO Madhav Bhonsle?"

"He is my PMO."

"Is that all Santosh? Or was there a personal relationship where he was paying you money? I have the bank statements, so please be careful with your reply," said Jugnu.

"Yes, there was. When Arjun was born, he did not look like me. He was fair while I was dark. I knew then that Arjun was not my son, but my love for Maya was so much that I forced myself to believe Arjun was my son. But when Arjun was six years old, Maya was ridden by guilt, and she confessed that you were, sorry, that Arjun was Madhav's son. I was devastated. My boss and my wife had betrayed me. I confronted Madhav and told him I would expose him to the world. Madhav got scared and bought my silence. He said he would pay me monthly for as long as I lived. But the moment you, sorry Arjun, went to jail, the payments stopped."

"So, he was paying you to keep his secret, but once Arjun was convicted, he became bold and stopped the payment."

"Yes," said Santosh.

"No more questions for now, your honour," said Jugnu

"Do you have any questions for Santosh?" Judge Mahmood asked Thambi.

"No questions," said Thambi.

"My lord, Santosh's testimony indicates that Madhav was lying. He knew Arjun was his son, as Santosh told him, and was bribing Santosh to keep his mouth shut. But Madhav wanted a permanent solution to this problem, not having Santosh like a Damocles sword over him. So, when an opportunity in the form of Arjun's arrest for Vijaya's rape presented itself, he took it and framed Arjun using fabricated medical reports and evidence," said Jugnu.

"This is all conjecture," shouted Thambi.

"Then prove otherwise," countered Jugnu, but Thambi did not respond.

Judge Mahmood looked at Thambi and Jugnu and said, "Gentlemen, we are not here to prove that Madhav framed Arjun. That has already been proved. We are here to find out who raped Vijaya. So, please focus on that."

Chapter 9

Jugnu continued, "Your honour, to give a clear perspective of what transpired and led to this heinous crime, we must go into everyone's past."

"Then please do," said Judge Mahmood.

Jugnu began his narration, "Your Honour, Vijaya was initially the daughter of Shanti and Kishan Kulkarni. Unfortunately, Kishan died tragically in a road accident while coming home one day from work. The car slipped off the road, fell sixty feet into the Ghats, and rose in flames. Nothing was left of the body or the vehicle. After giving Shanthi a month to grieve, Madhav Bhonsle, a known womaniser, moved into Shanthi's life, saying he was a friend of Kishan. Soon, he made Shanthi fall for him and married her. Shanthi and young Vijaya moved into Madhav's house. As time went by, Shanthi realised that Madhav was a womaniser and was having affairs with many women. She confronted and fought with him but could not leave him as Madhav had complete control over all her wealth by then. Shanthi and Vijaya would have been on the streets without food, clothing and shelter. So, she compromised and suffered quietly."

"When Madhav learned of the relationship between Arjun and Vijaya, he was livid. The reason was disgusting. Madhav had eyes on Vijaya as well. Shanthi knew this; hence, she encouraged the relationship between Arjun and Vijaya. A frustrated and desperate

Madhav was looking for a chance to get me out of the picture. With me gone, he would have hit two birds with one stone. On one hand, he could have Vijaya; on the other, the payments to blackmailer Santosh could be stopped. Madhav was the happiest man when Vijaya got raped because it allowed him to frame Arjun, which he did."

"The question remains, who raped Vijaya?" asked Judge Mahmood.

"Yes, Your Honour. For that, I would like to call Santosh to the stand again," said Jugnu.

The bailiff called out to Santosh, who retook the stand.

Jugnu looked at Santosh and asked, "When did you start hating Arjun?"

"From the time he was born. I suspected him not being my child from the first time I saw him," said Santosh.

"Then, one day, Maya told you Arjun was Madhav's child."

"Yes, I was devastated and would have left, but I loved her, so I swallowed my pride and continued."

"And you continued hating Arjun."

"Yes. After Maya's death, I stopped hating. Because I just stopped caring for the boy."

"You left a toddler to survive by himself?"

"He is still alive, grown, and has become a big fat lawyer, hasn't he?" asked Santosh.

Jugnu looked at Santosh and said, "You hated Arjun because he was Madhav's child, but you hated Madhav more because he stole the woman you loved."

"Oh, yes, I did."

"And you hated Madhav more when Maya left you."

"I wanted to kill him when Maya committed suicide. Maya died, not because of the guilt; she died the day she came to know he had dumped her and married Shanthi. She always thought it would only be her if he were to marry because she believed he loved only her. Finding out that he loved Shanthi so much that they were marrying each other was too much for her. So, she committed suicide."

"So, you confronted him with everything. You told him you have proof that she had committed suicide because of him, which was enough to send him to jail."

"Yes,"

"So, more than being known as the father of a bastard, he was worried you would expose him as the reason for Maya's death, right?"

"Yes,"

"And then he stopped paying. Why did you not retaliate?"

"I wanted to, but his friend SHO Gaitonde called me and threatened me. He said if I opened my mouth on anything, he would have me killed in an encounter," said Santosh.

"But you wanted to take revenge."

"Yes"

"So, you decided to destroy his daughter, Vijaya," said Jugnu.

"Yes... no, no," Santosh stuttered, but the cat was out of the bag.

Jugnu handed a piece of paper to Judge Mahmood and Thambi and said, "This is the signed confession of the bar dancer Shivani. One day, Santosh was so drunk that he blurted everything out to her. This statement tells you everything, Your Honour." Jugnu turned to Santosh and said, "You knew Arjun was Vijaya's tutor and that raping Vijaya would destroy not only Madhav but also his bastard son Arjun who was in love with her. Madhav destroyed your wife and future, so you decided to ruin his life and future. Little did you know that Madhav never considered Shanti and Vijaya to be his family. He married Shanthi only for her money."

"The story is good, but where is the proof?" asked Thambi.

Jugnu handed Maya's diary to Judge Mahmood, saying, "It is Maya Pallav's dying testimony, Your Honour. That night, when she jumped into the Ajara River to commit suicide, she was rescued by a good doctor. A kind man called Dr Arun Chandavarkar, whom Maya later married. She did not want Santosh to know she was alive, so she stayed hidden. Everyone took care of themselves and left Arjun to fend for himself, but in their old age, they all returned to help him. Maya kept records of everything in the diary and recorded her statement before a judge, who signed and notarized it. Shivani, Shanthi, and SHO Gaitonde submitted similar statements. I presume it was written in Arjun's destiny to suffer the first half of his life so that he appreciates the value of life in the second half. But what stands out is that some goodness left in all of them helped Arjun solve this crime."

Jugnu turned to Santosh, saying, "You ruined Vijaya's and Arjun's life to avenge your ruin. Two innocent people went through pain, suffering and trauma because of you. Your revenge is complete. At least now accept that you are guilty."

The courtroom was silent, waiting for Santosh to respond. Finally, Santosh looked at Jugnu and said, "Yes, I raped Vijaya Bhonsle."

The following morning, Jugnu and Vinathi were having breakfast. The newspaper lay on the table, and the headlines read, *"Dasara Vakil – Jugnu Joshi strikes again. Santosh Bangar and Madhav get life sentences."*

Chapter 10

Two days had passed since the court sent Santosh and Madhav to Dasara jail. Vinathi was reading a copy of Maya's diary that Jugnu had made for himself. In the diary, Maya details how she, a young nurse, met with Madhav in the hospital and how he wooed her with gifts and a promise of marriage. Then, when she was one month pregnant, he dumped her. Afraid she would be humiliated in society, she panicked and tried to end her life, but her roommate advised her to quickly get married and show the baby as a premature delivery. The roommate identified Santosh, who had a crush on her. And since he came from the same caste as her, her parents agreed. Eight months later, she delivered Arjun.

Unable to get over Madhav, she remained aloof most of the time, but deep inside, she still believed that Madhav would marry her. The news of Madhav marrying Shanthi was devastating and Maya tried to commit suicide but, was unlucky. Dr Arun Chandavarkar rescued her and took her to Mumbai. In Arun, she found true love and married him, but they decided to keep her past a secret. Sitting in Mumbai, she could not track Arjun. Everywhere, his name had changed to Jugnu. As the years passed, she gave up hope and continued living in Mumbai. Then the court hearings started, and she realised Jugnu was Arjun. She wanted to reach out to him but was afraid that filled with hate, he would reject her. A few years ago, Arun died due to COVID, and she contracted cancer. She maintained everything in the diary and even recorded her statements in front of a judge, hoping that it may all help Arjun after her time. Then she saw a bulletin in the paper that mentioned Joshi had adopted Jugnu. Maya asked her lawyer to contact Joshi so that she could tell him everything. Joshi arrived with Jugnu. The last page read, "Forgive me Arjun for I have sinned. Your ever-loving mother, Maya."

Epilogue

Vinathi was going through some files when she heard Jugnu speaking to Vijaya. "Yes, Vijaya, your father did not die in a car accident; He was murdered, and I have an eyewitness."

370 kms away, Joshi sat with Police Commissioner Rakesh Maria in his office in Mumbai.

"A critical case has come up about a criminal you have dealt with before. Please handle it. SP Gaikwad will take over from you. Once you have completed the Dasara jail handover, report to the Crime HQ in Crawford market. DCP Suresh Chavanke is waiting for you," said Rakesh.

"When do you want me to take charge, sir?" asked Rakesh

"Today, Joshi, today. A Scorpio SUV has been assigned to you. It is waiting outside," said Rakesh as he got up.

"But sir, I have not even informed Gomathi."

"Don't worry. I have informed her, and she has no issues. In fact, she is arriving today to see the government quarters. She is carrying some of your clothes and your old uniform. I believe the new quarters are excellent."

"But sir, I need to ..." Joshi tried to argue his case, but by then, Rakesh had already left.

Joshi shook his head in disbelief, walked out, got into his Scorpio and drove off to Crawford Market.

***

Acknowledgements

We express our deepest gratitude to Anish Chandy. Your vision, guidance, and unwavering belief in our work have been instrumental in bringing this book to life. Your guidance and support have meant more to us than words can convey, and we are truly fortunate to have you by our side.

A heartfelt thank you to our exceptional team at Srishti Publishers & Distributors. Your keen eye for detail, insightful feedback, and dedication to refining our words have elevated this book in ways we could never have imagined. Your commitment and passion for this project made the entire process rewarding. This book is as much a result of your hard work as ours. Thank you for helping us shape our vision into reality.